BBC

DOCTOR WHO

The Shining Man

Also available from BBC Books:

DIAMOND DOGS
by Mike Tucker

PLAGUE CITY
by Jonathan Morris

BBC

DOCTOR WHO

The Shining Man

Cavan Scott

BBC
BOOKS

1 3 5 7 9 10 8 6 4 2

BBC Books, an imprint of Ebury Publishing
20 Vauxhall Bridge Road,
London SW1V 2SA

BBC Books is part of the Penguin Random House group of companies whose
addresses can be found at global.penguinrandomhouse.com

Penguin
Random House
UK

First published by BBC Books in 2017

www.eburypublishing.co.uk

Editorial Director: Albert DePetrillo
Copyeditor: Steve Tribe
Series consultant: Justin Richards
Cover design: Lee Binding © Woodlands Books Ltd, 2017
Production: Alex Merrett

A CIP catalogue record for this book is available from the British Library

ISBN 9781785942686

Printed and bound in Great Britain by Clays Ltd, St Ives PLC

Penguin Random House is committed to a sustainable future for
our business, our readers and our planet. This book is made
from Forest Stewardship Council® certified paper.

For Mark

Chapter 1

Making it up

'Mum!'

Sammy Holland was barely through the front door before her son ran the length of the hallway and threw his arms around her.

'Hey, what's all this?' she said, prising Noah away from her waist and dropping down to look into his puffy eyes. She wiped a tear away from his cheek. 'Whatever's happened?'

Noah was 8 and short for his age, with a freckled face, chipmunk-like cheeks and a mop of curly brown hair. He sniffed, wiping snot on the back of his hand. 'It jumped out at me and Frankie. It was horrible.'

Sammy frowned. 'What did? What are you talking about?'

'He's making it up!' came a voice from the lounge.

Sammy looked across the hall. Through the lounge door, she could see her daughter draped over the sofa. Ten going on eighteen, Masie took after her father, more's the pity. The two children couldn't have been more different. While Noah was short, Masie was long and willowy, her

7

shoulder-length hair poker straight and so dark it was almost black. Their temperaments were just as distinct. Noah was the quintessential mummy's boy, always looking for a hug, while Masie was becoming a thoroughly independent miss, desperate to grow up. She was all about make-up, celebrity gossip and being glued to her mobile phone 24-7.

'Making up what?' Sammy asked. 'Will someone tell me what's been going on? Why's your brother so upset?'

'Is that you, love?' a woman's voice called out from the back of the house. 'Am I glad you're home!'

'Mum?' Dropping her handbag by the door, Sammy scooped Noah into her arms and carried him through to the kitchen, his tears running down her neck. Her mum was in the utility room, piling wet clothes into the tumble dryer. Sammy didn't know how she'd manage without her. She'd retired early, giving up her job at the local Co-op to help look after the kids. She picked them up from school every day, giving them their tea, so Sammy didn't have to rush home early from work. Of course, Sammy had told her time and time again that she didn't have to do the laundry, but Hilary Walsh was not the kind of woman who took no for an answer; or put up with nonsense from her grandkids for that matter.

'I haven't been able to do anything with him since we got back from school,' Hilary said, rubbing her back as she slammed the dryer shut.

Sammy sat Noah on the worktop, as she had whenever they needed a serious chat ever since he was a toddler. He sat swinging his legs, looking down at the checked lino on the floor, refusing to even meet her gaze.

'OK. Let's have it. Who jumped out at you, Noah?'

Hilary crossed her arms and gave her grandson a knowing look. 'If you don't tell her, I will.'

Noah still didn't respond. Sammy's Mum tutted.

'All right, then,' she said. '*Someone* decided to leave the school grounds at lunchtime.'

Sammy's hands went to her hips. 'Noah, you didn't!'

'Do you want to tell her why?'

Noah mumbled something incoherently. Sammy took a step back and, mirroring her mother, crossed her own arms. She didn't like to admit it, but the two of them were like peas in a pod. Neither woman was taller than five foot four, both had tight curly hair and blue-green eyes, and they shared a contempt for lies and liars.

'Sorry?' Sammy asked, jutting her head forward. 'What was that?'

Noah sighed and gave into the inevitable. 'It was Dylan. He said he'd seen one on the way to school, down Shrewfoot Avenue.'

'Seen what?'

Noah wiped his eye with the heel of his hand, still looking everywhere other than at his mum. 'A Shining Man,' he mumbled.

'You're kidding me.' Sammy looked from the boy to her mother, who just shrugged and shook her head. 'That nonsense on the radio? What have I told you about leaving the school? What did Mr Weenink say?'

'Oh, he said enough, trust me,' Hilary said, before explaining in excruciating detail how disappointed the new head teacher had been.

'I don't believe it,' Sammy said, running her hands through her hair, still damp from the rain. She stomped back into the kitchen and flicked the kettle on. She didn't want a cup of anything; it was just habit. Something to do other than rant at her son. Of all the stupid things to do. 'A Shining Man? Really?'

Noah followed her out. 'But Dylan was right. We saw him.'

'Told you he was making it up,' Masie shouted from the other room.

'Not helpful,' Sammy called back. 'And get off that screen. Haven't you got homework to do?'

'Done it already,' came the reply. 'I'm skyping Shona.'

Sammy went to respond, but stopped herself. *Choose your battles, Sammy. Choose your battles.*

Blowing air from her cheeks, she led Noah to the kitchen table and sat him down.

'Noah,' she said, sitting beside him and taking his hand. 'Shining Men don't exist. They're just some silly urban legend that's got out of hand.'

Noah looked puzzled. 'What's an urban legend?'

'A story that's told to scare people.'

'But Dylan said—'

'Dylan Edwards says a lot of things,' she snapped. 'All of them rubbish.' She paused, regaining her composure. 'Why were you *really* out of school? Were you going to the newsagent?'

'I told you. We were looking for the Shining Man, but he found us first. He jumped out of the bush and roared at us.'

'Noah...'

He yanked his hand away. 'Frankie said you wouldn't believe me, and he's right.'

'I didn't say—'

'It happened!' Noah insisted. 'His eyes shined right in our faces, we couldn't see anything, and he tried to grab Frankie.'

'And you told Mr Weenink this?'

'I've told *everyone*, but no one's listening.' The chair squeaked on the kitchen floor as Noah pushed it away and bolted from the room. Sammy let her head drop into her hands and listened to the thud-thud-thud of her son charging upstairs.

'You shouldn't let him talk at you like that,' Hilary said from the sink, the sound of the water running into the bowl competing with the music now blasting from Noah's room upstairs.

'Leave that, Mum,' Sammy said, standing up. 'I'll do it later.' She undid her coat and went to hang it beneath the stairs. 'What if he's telling the truth?'

Hilary snorted. 'About seeing ghosts and goblins? You're as soft as he is if you believe that.'

'*Something's* scared him.'

'Yeah, being caught out of school. He's talking bobbins, and you know it.'

Sammy leant against the kitchen door and sighed. The Shining Men. She'd laughed when she'd first heard about them. Bogeymen spotted on street corners, turning up on blurry photos, two blazing lights for eyes. She'd seen the pictures online, like something from the cheap horror films Noah's dad used to make her watch. It was the same every week. A new DVD would plop through the door with a garish cover and a stupid name, and she'd have to pretend she enjoyed every gory minute. *The Devil's Whisper. The Walls Have Teeth. Children of the Cull.* What a load of rubbish. If she never saw another monster movie, it would be too soon.

She'd dismissed the early Shining Man reports as a publicity stunt for a similarly puerile film. Halloween was just around the corner, after all. But then the kids started banging on about Shining Men at school, freaking each other out, claiming to have seen them hanging around the neighbourhood. And Dylan-blooming-Edwards was the worst of the lot. That boy wouldn't know the truth if it bit him on the bum.

'Mu-uuum!' Masie whined from the lounge. 'Noah's playing his music too loud. I can't hear Shona!'

'It's *not* too loud!' Noah shouted back down the stairs, and whacked the stereo up at least another ten decibels.

Sammy fought the urge to bang her head against the wall. It was going to be a long night.

Two hours later and the atmosphere in the Holland household had mellowed considerably. Masie was in her room, probably still glued to a screen, while Sammy perched on the side of Noah's bed, a well-thumbed book in her hands.

'The goblin hopped up and down in anger,' she read. '"It's a trick," it complained. "A filthy trick by a filthy human."'

Noah giggled. He always loved it when she did the goblin's squeaky voice.

'Jack smiled at the imp,' she continued. '"We made a deal," he reminded the creature, "and I've kept my half of the bargain. Now it's time to keep yours."

'"You haven't heard the last of me," the goblin snarled, disappearing in a puff of smoke. In its place was a golden egg. Jack scooped up his prize and ran all the way home where he and his mother lived happily ever after."'

Noah smiled, nestled beneath his superhero duvet; the Ghost soaring up, up and away across a Manhattan skyline. 'Thanks, Mum.'

She brushed a lock of hair back from his forehead. 'You're welcome.'

'Can I read for a bit?'

She closed the book and handed it over. 'Half an hour and then lights off. And I'll be up to check.'

He nodded, already flicking through the brightly coloured pages to find a story to read. Not that he didn't know them all off by heart. Sammy had lost count of the times they'd read it together, but she didn't mind. *The Goblins of Neverness* had been a favourite of hers since she was little. Back then it had been her dad doing the funny voices, making her squeal with laughter every time the goblin was outraged.

She leant over and planted a kiss on Noah's head. 'Love you, peanut.'

'Love you too, Mum.'

Sammy left him to his fairy tales, checking in on Masie. As expected, her daughter was watching YouTube videos on her bed, headphones clamped firmly over her ears. Sammy just couldn't understand it. Masie spent more time watching other kids playing computer games than playing them herself. Still, anything for a quiet life. At least she wasn't squabbling with her brother.

Sammy went downstairs. The radio was still playing in the kitchen. A hit from the 1990s. Sammy smiled. Her mum had always hated that one, played over and over on loop.

She walked into the kitchen, flicking on the kettle as she passed. The tea things were still in the sink. Usually her mum would have done them, but she had rushed into town to see a show at the Palace with the girls from bingo. Sammy laughed to herself. *The Girls.* Not one of them was under 60.

The song on the radio finished to be replaced by the seven o'clock news. Sammy already knew what the first headline would be. The same story had been rehashed for every bulletin since she'd got home.

'*Shining Man arrested in Stockport,*' the newsreader declared. '*Locals demand action.*'

Sammy sighed and switched off the radio. She'd heard enough about Shining Men for one night, thank you very much. This was getting out of control. Now people were dressing up as the damned things just to scare people. The guy in Stockport had been caught jumping out at an 82-year-old woman, giving her the fright of her life. Sicko. The thought of someone doing that to Noah made her blood boil. Masie was convinced he'd made it all up, but Noah had stuck to his guns all evening. Sammy didn't know what to believe. At least he'd think twice before slipping out of school again.

Sammy's mobile rang, out in the hallway. She went to recover it from her handbag, glancing at the screen. It was Polly from work. She clicked answer.

'Hiya Pol,' she said, wandering back to the kitchen. The kettle had stopped boiling and she flicked it on again, finding a clean mug from the draining rack. 'No, I can't get out tonight. Mum's gone into town, so there's no one to watch the kids.' Polly made a suggestion and Sammy scoffed. 'Yeah, like that'll happen. You know Mike. He needs at least two months' notice to see his own children. Besides, Noah needs me around tonight.'

She dropped a teabag into the mug, telling Polly about the entire Shining Man debacle. She poured the water and went to get milk from the fridge. 'I know. It's all over the news. Did you hear about the bloke in Stockport? Should throw away the key.'

She returned to the sink, glancing up as she slopped milk into her tea. 'I don't believe it.'

In her ear, Polly asked her what was wrong.

'There's one on the corner of the street. A Shining Man!'

Polly swore in response.

'Not a "real" one, obviously. One of those nutters dressing up.'

Sammy leaned across the sink to get a closer look. The figure was tall and painfully thin, its back to her. As she watched, it turned its head and two beams of light swept across the road in front of it.

'It must be wearing head torches or something,' she muttered, prompting Polly to ask what she'd said.

'Nothing,' she replied, making a decision. 'Pol, I've got to go.' She stormed out of the kitchen, snatching her coat from the peg in the wall. 'I'm not going to let them get away with this, frightening innocent people.'

On the phone, Polly tried to dissuade her. 'What are they going to do to me?' Sammy said, slipping on her coat. 'Probably a big coward behind all that get up, anyway. Yeah, yeah. I'll be careful. I call you back.'

Sammy ended the call, looking around for her keys. Where were they?

She rifled through her pockets, putting her phone down on the bookcase in the hall. She walked back into the kitchen, spotting her keyring by the kettle, the little plastic pixie from a family holiday to Cornwall winking cheekily at her.

She grabbed the keys, heading back to the door.

'Just stepping out for a moment,' she yelled up to the kids, opening the front door. 'Stay in bed.' She didn't wait for either of them to reply.

The cold hit her as soon as she stepped outside. What kind of freak stands around on street corners in the middle of October? Probably, the same kind of low-life that jumps out at kiddies near schools. Zipping up her coat, Sammy marched down the road.

'Oi,' she cried out. 'What do you think you're doing?'

The figure didn't turn. They didn't even flinch, standing there in their long shabby coat, greasy hair stretching down their back.

'I'm talking to you!' she continued. 'It isn't right, what you're doing. Scaring people. It's not a joke, you know? My little boy was terrified earlier today. Really, really scared.'

Still the weirdo ignored her. She wasn't having that.

She couldn't tap him on the shoulder. The guy was too tall for that. Ridiculously tall. But even that didn't stop her, not today. Sammy grabbed him by the arm, pulling him around to face her.

'Well, what have you got to say for yourself?'

The Shining Man didn't say anything, but he did turn, the light from his torches dazzling her. Sammy threw up a hand. 'Hey. Cut it out. Turn those things off.'

The figure tilted its strangely elongated head, and Sammy's words died in her throat. The light wasn't streaming from torches, but from wide blazing eyes. The thing in front of her had no nose, no ears, no features at all. That had to be a mask. Yes, that's what it was, just better than the cheap Halloween tat they sold at Betterworths.

All the same, Sammy took a step back as a slit appeared across the void of a face. The slit opened to become a gaping mouth that shined bright in the darkness.

Sammy stumbled, and then screamed as the light washed over her, blotting out everything else, burning her skin.

And then the Shining Man closed its eyes and ragged mouth, and the face was smooth once again.

The figure disappeared, flickering out of view.

Curtains twitched in number fifteen, one of Sammy's neighbours looking out.

17

They'd heard something. Had it been a scream? No. The street was empty. It must have been a cat.

Back in her house, Sammy's mobile rang where she had left it on the bookcase. Noah ran down the stairs and picked it up. It was Polly, his Mum's friend.

'No, she's not here,' he told the woman. 'She said she had to pop out.'

He opened the door and looked outside, but there was no sign of his mum.

Sammy Holland had disappeared.

Chapter 2

Stormy Weather

Bill's life was mad. One hundred per cent, no messing about, certifiably mad.

It hadn't always been like this. Not until she got a job at the university. Serving chips in the canteen. Sounded simple enough.

Then she started sneaking into the lecture halls, listening to what the professors had to say. One soon became her favourite, but he wasn't a professor. He was a doctor. *The* Doctor.

No one knew what subject he was supposed to be teaching. Some said it was physics. Others claimed it was history. But Bill didn't care. Each lecture was different, covering everything under the sun. The Doctor taught art, and literature, and action figures, and music. He talked about comics, and philosophy, and computing, and architecture, and knitting, and engineering, and … stuff. Lots and lots of stuff. But he never made any of it seem trivial. Sitting in his lecture hall, listening to him speak, you couldn't help but be swept along by his words, by his enthusiasm. To the Doctor, a bag of jelly babies was just as fascinating as quantum mechanics. Everything was connected. Everything was important.

Then he had made her an offer. Sitting behind his desk in his office.

Actually, it was more of an ultimatum.

'If you ever get less than a First, it's over ...'

She hadn't a clue what he was talking about, but he continued anyway.

'A First. Every time. Or I stop immediately.'

'Stop what?' she'd asked, and then he'd said it. Four magic words.

'Being your personal tutor.'

It was still hard to believe. Bill Potts, server of chips, had her own personal tutor, someone who believed in her enough to share the secrets of the universe.

Literally.

Because her personal tutor turned out to be an alien with a time machine in his study. A time machine that looked like a police box on the outside and was bigger on the inside. A time machine that could go anywhere in history, if it wanted to. Bill had been to the future. She'd been to the past. She'd run from killer robots and eaten alien fish. But none of that was the mad bit.

The mad bit was how natural it all felt. How *right*.

Even standing here, in an impossible time machine owned by a 2,000-year-old nutter, Bill felt like she belonged. Like she was safe.

That was, of course, until the TARDIS was hit by a storm. Not outside. Oh no. That would be too normal for the Doctor. Too boring. No, this storm hit *inside*.

It came without warning. The Doctor was working at the console as usual. He was tall and thin, with a shock of grey hair and eyebrows that could stop a supernova in its tracks. His wardrobe ranged from ageing punk rocker to sharp-suited mod, but today veered towards the latter: a crisp white shirt buttoned to the neck beneath a velvet Crombie jacket.

His fingers were dancing over the controls of his ship, the console beeping and chiming in time with whatever buttons he pressed in a sequence that was anyone's guess. There was nothing particularly odd in this, except for perhaps the potted plant he had balanced beside the central column. That was new. Perhaps he wanted to pretty the place up a bit, although the blue and yellow blooms would be less precarious on one of the many reading tables dotted around the upper gantry.

Bill was considering all this when the wind started to pick up. It was barely noticeable at first, like a breeze from an open door. Then it grew. The Doctor didn't even seem to notice, until it began whistling around the upper level, the walls of the TARDIS creaking as if at sea.

He glanced up as papers swirled from above, carried by a gust of wind that rushed down the stairs. The deck shuddered beneath Bill's feet, before bucking like a fairground ride, throwing her against the console. Opposite her, the Doctor made a grab for the plant.

She barely heard the pot smash on the floor above the roar of the gale.

'Aren't you going to ask me?' the Doctor shouted from where he was hanging from a particularly flimsy-looking lever.

'Ask you what?' she yelled back.

'People usually ask me what's happening when the TARDIS is attacked.'

'We're being *attacked?*'

'You noticed!' the Doctor said, as a large leather-bound book flew from one of the shelves on the upper walkway to almost take off his head. 'I knew you would.'

The heavy-looking volume bounced once on the floor before being snatched back up into the whirlwind.

'It's kind of hard to miss!' Bill said as something slapped against her cheek. She cried out before realising it was just a dog-eared children's book.

'Hey, that's a first edition,' the Doctor complained as she chucked it onto the floor. '*Little Miss Sunshine versus the Sulky Skarasen*. I helped with the pictures.'

'Doctor!'

'What?'

'The attack?'

'Oh yes, that.' he said, turning his attention back to the controls. 'Nothing to worry about. Everything's completely under control.'

'I'd hate to see it when it's not. Ow!'

'Now what?' he asked, his jacket billowing out behind him.

'Something hit me.' Bill rubbed her hand, yelping as she was struck again, this time behind her ear.

'What kind of something?'

'Something hard.'

A tiny ball of ice bounced off the console in front of her.

'Is that … is that *hail*?' she asked, making the mistake of looking up as the deluge began in earnest. Hailstones the size of marbles hammered down, clattering on the deck and stinging her skin like a thousand tiny pinpricks.

'This is not supposed to happen,' the Doctor announced as the console began to spark and fizz beneath the meteorological assault.

'No kidding!'

There was a crash from below, a clatter that could have only been the Doctor's precious guitar toppling from its stand. He shot a mournful look down the stairs before redoubling his efforts with the controls.

'Have you got an umbrella?' he asked, wiping icy water from his eyes as he worked.

'Of course I haven't!'

'Then bring one next time. Useful things, brollies. Always used to carry one, back when I was Scottish the first time around.'

'You're babbling,' she told him, her fingers now numb with the cold. 'You always babble when you're scared.'

'I'm never scared!' he snapped, throwing a lever without warning. The room lurched, and Bill fell away, not because she let go of the console or even slipped. Instead, she was grabbed and pulled from her feet.

Grabbed by a hand that wasn't there.

A hand with claws.

She skidded across the room, smacking her head on the TARDIS doors … and the storm stopped.

It was that quick. One minute the wind was raging, books were flying and the hail was falling, and then next … everything was as it should be – other than the Doctor fussing over her.

'Bill? Bill, can you hear me?'

'Y-yeah. Of course I can.'

He looked at her with concern written all over his craggy features. 'How many heads am I holding up?'

'Don't you mean fingers?'

He stood, offering her his hand. 'You've never met my godmother.'

She stood, gazing at the carnage all around the control room. 'What happened to the wind and stuff?'

'Oh, that,' the Doctor said, waving away the question as he returned to the console. 'I turned it off.'

'You turned off a storm …'

'It wasn't actually a storm,' he told her, picking up books to stack them in almost neat piles on the stairs. 'Not really.'

'Felt like one to me,' she replied, lending a hand. It was odd. Books, maps, papers and a document claiming to be the last will and testament of Lord Lucan were strewn across the floor, but none of them were wet. She'd at least expected the deck to be dusted by a thin layer of hailstones, but they were gone. There weren't even any puddles.

'It was certainly unexpected,' the Doctor agreed, as he climbed up to the upper gantry to return his blackboard to its easel from where it had fallen. 'Sorry about that.'

'It wasn't your fault.'

The Doctor avoided her gaze as he skipped back down to the console.

'It *was* your fault?'

'Not exactly,' he said, putting the console between them, just in case. 'Well, maybe a little. I was running some tests.'

She circled the control panels to face him. 'What kind of tests?'

'The telepathic circuits,' the Doctor said, glancing towards a row of slimy rubberised ridges on a nearby panel.

'The TARDIS is telepathic?'

'Everything's a little telepathic. Except squirrels. No one knows why. Especially the squirrels.'

'So what were you testing?'

The Doctor glanced at the shattered remains of his pot plant. Bill's mouth dropped open. 'You were testing a *flower*?'

'Not just any flower,' the Doctor told her, scooping up the plant and looking for somewhere to deposit it. 'A primrose. Incredible plants, primroses. By the late fifty-fourth century, they evolve into a race of brilliant philosophers and orators. Minds the like of which the galaxy has never seen.' He slapped the pile of earth, petals and bent stems unceremoniously into Bill's hands. 'Here, hold on to this.'

Soil slipped between her fingers.

The Doctor returned to the console. 'I was trying to detect that guy's thoughts. His name's Nigel, by the way.'

Bill gaped at the battered flower. 'The primrose is called Nigel ...'

'Or Martin,' the Doctor said, checking the scanner screen. 'Or maybe George. Anyway, whatever his name, it turns out he doesn't have many thoughts that don't involve Grimsby Town Football Club.'

She raised a sceptical eyebrow. 'Now you're just taking the mickey.'

The Doctor nodded furiously. 'I know! Did you see their last match? Who in their right mind plays 3-5-2 against Barnet?'

'Doctor!'

He waved her towards the piles of books on the stairs. 'Just pop him over there.'

Bill almost apologised to the flower as she did what she was told. 'So, these tests …'

'Proved slightly trickier than I expected. I was forced to drop the TARDIS's psionic defence grid …'

'Opening us to attack.'

The Doctor gave her an appreciative grin. 'You're catching on.'

He pulled the display around to show her, as if she had a hope in hell of understanding the swirling circles that danced across the screen.

'Nope, sorry,' she admitted. 'Still need the Idiot's Guide. Where did the attack come from?'

He raised a long finger. 'Hold that thought.'

'Why? Where are you going?' she asked as he disappeared down to the lower level.

'Just a minute!'

'But, you don't understand,' she said, brushing soil from her palms as she walked to the top of the stairs. 'It wasn't just the storm. Something grabbed me.'

'Grabbed you?' he repeated, running back up to her, his black and white electric guitar in hand.

'Like a claw. It dragged me across the floor.'

'Interesting,' he said, giving the guitar's paintwork a cursory inspection before handing the instrument over to Bill. 'Look after that.'

She regarded him with extreme suspicion as he braced himself against the console. 'Why? What are you going to do?'

'This!' he announced, slamming his hand down hard on a button.

It was all back in an instant. The hail. The wind. Even the low-flying books.

'Seriously?' she asked, buffeted by winds that had no business to be there. 'This is your plan?'

'Works for me.' the Doctor replied. 'I stopped the storm by raising the defences.'

'So you've dropped them again?'

Thunder roiled high across the ceiling. The Doctor glanced up, looking as though he was loving every terrifying moment. 'I wonder if we'll get lightning this time?'

So much for feeling safe in the TARDIS.

'Just protect that guitar!' the Doctor instructed her as his fingers went to work on the controls.

'Forget the guitar. What about me?'

'A little hail never hurt anyone,' the Doctor insisted, flinching even as he said it. 'I just need to lock on to whoever's reaching out to us.'

'Reaching out? Is that what you call it? '

Bill's words were lost on the wind. She was blown back, lifted from her feet by a fresh squall. She crashed into the railing, still clutching the Doctor's precious guitar. This was ridiculous. Screwing up her face, she fought against the wind, stalking back to the console, even as the Doctor let out a cheer.

'Yes! Well done you.'

Bill heaved the guitar onto the console and smiled at the compliment, despite the weather. 'Don't mention it.'

Confusion flashed across the Doctor's face. 'I was talking to the TARDIS!'

He yanked down a lever and the time machine quaked to the sound of its own engines. 'She's picked up the scent!'

Chapter 3

A Cry for Help

'No, still no sign of her, love. The kids are going spare.'

Hilary had snatched the phone from its cradle as soon as it rang, her shoulders slumping when she realised it wasn't her daughter on the other end of the line.

It had become a familiar ritual these few days.

'Yeah. I will, love. But I'm fine, really. Got everything in hand.'

At the very least she'd hoped it would be PC Schofield, from Huckensall Police Station, but it never was. Just the latest in a long line of well-wishers – or out-and-out busybodies like Gracie Noakes.

'Thanks for phoning, Gracie love. Bye then. Bye.'

The handset beeped as it slotted back into the cradle. Hilary glanced up at the clock in the hallway, and willed herself not to cry. No more tears. There had been enough shed since Thursday, ever since she'd got out of the Palace Theatre to find seventeen missed calls on her mobile. Poor Masie had been so scared on the phone:

'Nan? Mum's gone out, and she hasn't come back. Can you call us, please?'

Masie tried to act so grown-up all the time, but Sammy's disappearance had only reminded Hilary how young her granddaughter still was.

Hilary plodded to the kitchen and stared at the kettle. How many times had she scolded Sammy for clicking it on whenever she walked into the kitchen? *It's just a habit, love. You hardly ever make a cup. Think of the electricity you're wasting.*

Sammy's dad had been the same. Continually boiling the kettle whether anyone wanted a brew or not.

Hilary couldn't give a monkeys about wasted electricity now. She just wanted her Sammy back.

She opened the blinds at the kitchen window, searching the dark street for any movement outside. The council had replaced the streetlights with those new LED lamps. They didn't give half as much light as the old ones. Far too gloomy, if you asked her. Hilary had told their local MP exactly what she thought of them at his last surgery down at the community centre. What was the point of saving the planet if the streets weren't safe?

That was a thought. Maybe their Right Honourable Waste of Space could help for once. She'd ring him first thing in the morning. Tomorrow would be three days since Sammy disappeared. The police would be passing the case onto the Missing People Unit, at least that's what PC Schofield said.

'Your daughter will be home in no time, Mrs Walsh. I'm sure of it.'

How on earth could she be sure, sitting there fresh-faced in her uniform, a mere slip of a girl?

It was true what they said. You know you're getting old when the police start to look younger.

They'd looked younger for a long time.

She took off her glasses and rubbed her eyes. Dropping them beside the kettle, she went to pull the blinds. That's when she saw it, something moving at the end of the street. Snatching up her glasses, Hilary rushed to the front door, flinging it open.

'Sammy?'

No such luck. It was just the tabby from number seven, the dirty little so-and-so that did its business beneath Sammy's bushes.

Hilary leant on the doorframe and let out a sob. She didn't care if any of the neighbours were watching, not this time.

'Where are you Sammy love?' she asked the night. 'Come home, won't you? Please.'

Upstairs, Noah tossed and turned in bed. He couldn't sleep, but there was no point going downstairs. Nan would only send him back to bed, quick-smart.

Mum wouldn't.

Mum would let him cuddle up with her on the sofa and watch the soaps. Not for long, mind. Just enough to make him feel sleepy.

But Mum wasn't here.

He turned over again, facing the wall as tears soaked his pillow. It wasn't fair. Why would Mum leave like that? Running out into the night, leaving her phone behind.

He was sure it was because of what he'd done, him and Frankie, sneaking out of school.

'*Don't be so soft, Noah-love,*' Nan had said, but he knew it was all his fault. Masie did too. He could tell the way she looked at him, from the blame in her eyes.

'Peanut?'

The voice made him jump. He twisted around, his duvet now one big knot. He couldn't see who had called out, but there was no mistaking the voice.

'Mum?'

'Peanut, I need you. I'm trapped.'

'Mum!'

Noah clawed the duvet away from his face. She was there, standing by the window, in the same clothes she'd been wearing the day she never came home. Her uniform from the Mercian Bank, a smart blouse and skirt, but even in the pale glow of his nightlight he could see they were dirty. The blouse was plastered with mud, like she'd been out playing rugby, her skirt ripped, rucked up over scabbed knees. Her hair was matted, leaves caught up in the curls he loved to twirl around his fingers, and her face was streaked, tears rolling down grimy cheeks.

'Noah, please … Can't get out.'

Noah kicked his duvet away, calling for his sister as another figure appeared behind Mum. It was tall, too tall, with long lank hair. And its *face* … It was completely blank, until it opened eyes that hadn't been there a second before, and light blazed across the room.

Noah couldn't move. It wasn't the duvet this time. His legs and arms just weren't working. He could only watch as the Shining Man wrapped its spindly arms around his mum and dragged her into a gaping hole in the floor. Sammy screamed and threw out an arm, reaching desperately for Noah, calling his name.

'Peanut, please! You've got to find us! Get us out of here!'

And then they were gone. Mum, the Shining Man, even the hole in the floor.

Noah finally found his voice, crying out as he tumbled from the bed, hitting the floor.

'Noah?'

The door of his bedroom flew open and Masie rushed in. She dropped beside him, scooping him up into her arms and forgetting for a moment that her role in life was to be on his case.

He hugged her back, holding her close. 'It was Mum. Masie, she was here. The Shining Man.'

'Shhh,' she said, stroking his tangled hair. 'It was just a bad dream.'

Now Nan appeared at the door. 'What's all the racket?'

'Noah had a nightmare,' Masie told her. 'That's all.'

Noah pushed his sister away. Why did she keep saying that? 'It wasn't a dream! She was here, by the window! A Shining Man got her. He dragged her into the floor!'

Masie looked where he was pointing, but Nan was having none of it.

'Enough of this now,' she said, smoothing out the crumpled duvet. 'I don't want to hear any more about Shining Men.'

'But ...'

She turned on him, angrily. 'But nothing. If you hadn't filled your mum's head with all this Shining Man nonsense—'

Nan stopped herself, but it was too late.

'She would never have gone out,' Noah barked, his eyes brimming with fresh tears.

Nan sagged against the bed, her face greyer than ever. 'I didn't mean—'

The phone rang in the hall. Nan went to go and then stopped herself, caught between the need to make peace with her grandson and to rush downstairs.

'I'll tuck him in, Nan,' Masie said. 'Don't worry.'

'Thanks, love,' the old woman said, flashing Noah a look full of regret before disappearing out of the door.

The two of them listened to the stairs creak as she hurried down to the phone. There was a clatter and then a beep, followed by an eager 'Hello?'

Then came a pause, and a disappointed sigh. 'Oh hello, Barbara. No, still nothing.'

Masie got up and closed Noah's door.

He bristled where he sat on the floor, hugging his knees. 'I knew she blamed me.'

'She doesn't,' Masie said, listening through the door.

'And you're just going to tell me I imagined it. But it wasn't a dream, or a nightmare, or anything. Mum was here!'

'By the window,' Masie said.

Noah wiped his nose on his onesie sleeve. 'She said she needed me; that she was trapped.'

Masie flicked the light switch, the big light coming on. Both turned to the window, the curtains moving slightly from the breeze. There was a crack in the double-glazing. Mum always said she would get it fixed.

Masie crept forward, stopping next to Noah's desk. He shuffled over to where she was looking.

Mum had put a new carpet down the last time Noah's room was decorated; a light tan colour. Nan had told her she was mad.

'*A colour like that in a boy's room? It'll be filthy in no time.*'

Now, both Noah and Masie were glad that Mum hadn't listened to her.

There was a muddy footprint on the carpet beneath the draughty window, too large for Noah.

A woman's footprint. *Mum's* footprint.

There was something else as well. A leaf, brown and brittle, its edges curled up with age.

'Mum had leaves in her hair,' Noah told Masie as she bent down and prodded it carefully, as if worried it would burst into flames.

'What tree's it from?' Masie asked, kneeling beside Noah.

'I don't know. An oak maybe?' He'd made a large collage of leaves in year three, labelling each type in turn. 'But you know what this means, don't you?'

'Mum *was* here,' Masie said, staring at the footprint. 'It wasn't just a dream.'

Noah sniffed again. Without thinking, Masie reached up to his desk and pulled a tissue from a box, passing it to him. He blew his nose noisily.

'So what do we do?' he said, chucking the screwed-up rag at the *Star Wars* bin beneath the table. It fell to the floor instead.

Masie's voice wobbled as she answered, although Noah could tell she was trying to sound brave. 'We wait for Nan to go to sleep, and then we go down to the woods.'

Noah's eyes went wide. 'In the dark?'

Masie shrugged. 'Where else are we going to find an oak tree? If that's where Mum is …'

Noah wanted to crawl back into bed, pull the duvet over his head and pretend none of this was happening, but the memory of Mum and the Shining Man was just too fresh. Too painful.

Peanut, I need you. I'm trapped. You've got to find me. Get me out of here.

Noah got up and opened his desk drawer, pulling out the toy torches Mum had given him last time they went camping. One was shaped like a lightsaber; the other had Superman flying up its handle.

He passed the Man of Steel to his sister. Superman wouldn't be scared. Superman would save his mum.

'You're right,' he told Masie, testing the battery on the lightsaber. 'Let's go and find her.'

Chapter 4

Into the Woods

Masie and Noah had played in Boggle Woods since they were little; first with Dad, when he was still at home, and then later with Mum. They could find the place blindfolded. Just walk to the end of their street, Bugs Close, cross Brownie Hill and tramp across the field where Masie played football every Sunday morning. Simple.

They came here all year round: in spring, when the ground was a carpet of swaying bluebells; in autumn, when leaves buried what little paths there were; and in winter, when the trees were bare, empty branches stretching out like witch's fingers.

Just this last summer, Mum had started to let them go to the woods on their own. There were rules, of course, strict rules. They had to be careful crossing the road. They were to keep out of the brook that ran along the bottom of the trees.

And, most importantly, under no circumstances were they to venture into the woods after dark.

It was dark now.

Very dark.

Noah had almost chickened out when Masie had opened the front door. He was convinced that Nan was going to hear them. She was only in the living room, after all, sleeping on the sofa bed.

But she had kept on snoring, even when Masie had accidentally dropped her keys.

The door clicked shut behind them. There was no going back now.

'We're going to be in so much trouble,' Noah whispered as they hurried along the road, parkas and wellies over their onesies.

'Not if we bring Mum home,' Masie told him.

The world seemed weird in the middle of the night. There was hardly any traffic on the roads and the street lamps had turned themselves off to conserve power. Noah wanted to switch on his torch, but Masie said no.

'Not until we're away from the houses. You know how nosey the neighbours are.'

'You sound like Nan. Besides, won't they be asleep by now?'

'We don't want to risk it.'

Sure enough, the curtains at number fifteen were drawn back, a light on in the lounge, but the large widescreen telly was playing to an empty room.

'They must have gone to the loo,' Masie said, grabbing Noah's hand. 'Come on.'

Looking both ways they ran across Brownie Hill, and headed for the gate to the playing field.

It swung on its hinges next to the building site where a large detached house was being built. The place was barely more than a shell, just walls and a roof, the windows and doors gaping holes that were covered by thick plastic sheets that flapped in the wind.

Now the torches went on, their beams stretching weakly across the field as the children ran for the line of forbidding trees. Maybe the batteries hadn't been as strong as he thought. Perhaps they should go back.

Noah felt a splash on his cheek. 'It's going to rain,' he moaned.

'Then put up your hood,' Masie replied. Like he was going to do what she said. She wasn't the grown-up here, no matter how old she thought she was, but, as the clouds broke high above them, he had little choice. The rain came, the hood went up and they plunged into the wood.

'It'll be dry in the trees,' Maisie promised.

It wasn't. Most of the trees had already shed their leaves. There wasn't nearly enough to stop the rain.

'Which ones are oaks?' Noah asked, sweeping his torch around in a circle. They couldn't see the playing field any more, as if the trees had crept up behind them when they weren't looking to block the way.

'How am I supposed to know?' Masie replied. 'You're the expert.'

He looked up, tracing the line of lower branches with his lightsaber torch. They were mostly bare, hardly any leaves at all.

'That's a birch,' he said excitedly, spotted a spindly leaf in the shape of a club, still hanging on to a twig.

'See! You should be on *Autumnwatch*!' She put on a voice, a silly impression of that bloke on the telly Mum pretended not to fancy, Chris something-or-other. '"Look at the leaves, Michaela. Just look at them."'

Noah laughed, stopping abruptly when there was a sharp crack from behind. He spun around, shining his lightsaber the way they'd been. 'What was that?'

Masie didn't reply, listening intently. The woods were quiet, save for the relentless drumming of the rain against the ground.

'Ma-sie ...' Noah whimpered, moving closer to her.

'S'nothing,' she said, a little too quickly. 'Just an animal.'

'What kind of animal?'

'A badger. Maybe a fox?'

That was it. The thought of coming face-to-face with a snarling fox was too much. 'I want to go home,' he demanded.

Masie shone the Superman torch in his face. 'We can't! Not until we've found Mum!'

He screwed up his eyes, looking away from the light. 'But what if it really *was* a dream?'

'A dream that leaves footprints?'

There wasn't an answer to that.

Masie squeezed his arm. 'She needs us, Noah. We've got to go on.' She swung the torch onto the ground, illuminating the carpet of rotting leaves beneath their boots. 'Any of these look like oak leaves?'

Hoping that Masie would think they were rain, Noah wiped tears from his eyes. 'I-I don't think so.'

'But what about that old tree down by the brook, the one with the rope?'

'Mum said we shouldn't go down there.'

'She said we shouldn't go *in* the brook. That's different.'

She'd already broken that rule anyway. Masie had discovered a makeshift swing hung from the large tree during the school holidays. Noah had been too short to even reach the rope, but she had managed a few tentative swings across the bubbling water before dropping in with a splash.

The path down to the brook was treacherous enough in daylight. You had to skid down a steep slope, hoping you didn't end up sitting in the stream. Noah wasn't sure that he could make it in the middle of the night, and said so.

'Then go back,' Masie told him sharply, losing her patience. 'But if there's even a chance that's where Mum is, I'm going to look.'

She turned and marched purposefully into the trees, the beam from the Superman torch bobbing between the thick trunks.

Noah glanced behind him, trying to work out if he could find his way home. Even if he could, he'd seen enough episodes of *Mystery Inc.* to know that bad things happen when the Scooby Gang split up.

'Masie, wait for me!' he called out, crashing after his sister.

It didn't take him too long to catch up. They trudged on in silence, until Masie stopped without warning. She just stood there, breathing heavily.

'What is it?' Noah asked.

'Didn't you hear that?'

He looked around, peering into the darkness. 'Hear what?'

'Something moved. Something big.'

Noah's bottom lip started to wobble. 'You said it was a fox.'

Masie reached out and slipped her gloved fingers into his. 'Maybe it's a deer?'

Ahead of them, two lights appeared between the trees. 'Or maybe not.'

Noah took a step back, pulling at his sister's hand. 'It's one of them. A Shining Man.'

Masie didn't budge. It was like she was rooted to the spot.

'Masie!'

The lights blinked off. Masie brought her torch up.

There was nothing there.

Noah squeezed her fingers. 'Masie, I don't like it.'

'Neither do I,' she admitted as the lights reappeared to their left.

The children spun around to face them. They were closer now. Much closer.

Masie backed away, pulling Noah with her, until they vanished again. 'Run,' she said and they turned, only to skid to a halt.

The lights were in front now, glaring bright. And they were moving, rushing towards them, a blood-curdling cry echoing through the trees.

This time Masie didn't tell him to run. She didn't have to. The children turned and fled deeper into the wood.

They didn't know which way they were running. They just knew they had to get away. The Shining Man was right behind them. They could hear its feet pounding the wet leaves, branches splintering as it crashed after them.

Their shadows stretched out in front of them, lit by the light of the Shining Man's eyes. Masie raced ahead, Noah calling after her.

And then something snatched at his jacket and he fell, screaming all the way.

Chapter 5

Pull to Open

Charlotte Sadler was glad she'd packed her waterproof phone case. The rain was coming down hard, the trees creaking ominously in the wind. She was soaked, she was cold, but boy, was she happy.

This was *brilliant*. Talk about atmosphere. She couldn't have planned it better. Finding the right spot, she held the phone in front of her and adjusted the monopod so she was in shot. Checking that the night vision filter was on, she cleared her throat and hit record.

'Welcome to Boggle Woods,' Charlotte began in a stage whisper, a lapel mic clipped discretely to her dark bomber jacket. 'It is quite literally a dark and stormy night. No one in their right mind would be out here in these conditions, but hey, you're watching Cryptogal-UK. What do you expect?'

As introductions go, it was a bit corny, but she'd go with it for now. She could always edit in something new. Keeping her eyes on the camera, Charlotte took a tentative step forwards, walking the path she'd scoped out earlier.

'This is going to be my best video yet, I guarantee it. I'm in Shining Man country. Yes, you've seen the videos, you've seen the photos, coming in from all over Britain … from all over the world … But nowhere have there been more sightings than here – Huckensall, near Manchester. This is Ground Zero, people, where it all began.'

She slipped, nearly losing her footing. She grabbed a branch, stopping herself from falling. That would play out well on screen, ramping up the tension.

'Sorry about that. As you can see; it's a little slippy underfoot.' She showed the camera the wet leaves on the floor. 'And, before you ask, I'm not talking about creeps in cosplay, but the real deal. Actual Shining Men, looming out of the dark.'

That was bordering on melodramatic, but her fans liked it when she went a bit Hammer Horror; the geekier ones, at least.

With the camera back on her face, she adjusted the head torch on her trademark beanie and wiped water from her eyes before continuing.

'I'm going to take you right into the heart of the wood.' She made a show of glancing over her shoulder, as if she'd heard something. She looked back to camera and gave her best nervous smile. 'I have to admit; I don't like it out here. It's a spooky place at the best of times and, as you can see by the weather, this definitely isn't the best of times. But that's fine. I know you're all with me in spirit, so let's go.'

Charlotte tapped the screen, flipping the camera forward to record the path ahead. Speaking in hushed tones, she brought the viewers up to date with the Shining

Man phenomenon, recommending her other videos if they wanted to find out more. She'd add links later in the edit.

After a while she fell silent, the camera recording her progress. Most of this would get cut, but she had to keep the camera running, just in case. If something was going to happen, she hoped it would be soon. While all this would make a great vlog, the rain was already seeping through her jacket. She couldn't remember the last time she'd been so cold.

Charlotte stopped. 'What was that?' she asked the phone, panning the camera around.

There had been a sound up ahead, a weird electronic chattering; quiet at first, but soon joined by a wheezing, grinding bellow that rose to a crescendo. She'd never heard anything like it.

She broke into a run, charging towards the noise. There was a light as well, a pulsing glow that flashed in time with the raucous growl; on and off, on and off, sending shadows skittering through the trees.

She skidded into a small clearing just as the light and sound show came to an abrupt conclusion with a tremulous, thundering *thump*.

The wood was silent again, the only sound the patter of the rain that fell on the large box that hadn't been there this afternoon when she'd explored Huckensall for filming locations.

It was tall, roughly the height of a telephone box and made of wood, painted dark blue. White light streamed from windows mounted at eye level. Charlotte peeked in, but couldn't see anything through the frosted glass.

Stepping back, she circled the box, sweeping her phone up and down so the camera could take in the square panels beneath the windows.

'OK guys, this is bizarre,' she whispered. 'I don't know where this box has come from, or even what it is. It certainly wasn't here earlier today.' She pitched the camera up to make out words that were printed white on black above the windows. 'Police Public Call Box, whatever that is. Some kind of mobile HQ? Seems a little pokey.'

She reached out, brushing her fingers against the wood, only to snatch them away again. 'It's *vibrating* ... like an electric current was running through it. What kind of wood can be electrified?'

There was a set of doors, with a handle. 'Well,' she said, summoning up the courage. 'Only one way to find out what's inside ...'

She yanked at the handle. It wouldn't budge.

'Locked,' she told the camera. 'But there's a smaller handle here.' She read the words printed on a white panel for the benefit of her viewers. '*Pull To Open. Police Telephone. Free for use of Public.* Well, I'm a member of the public, so ...'

She pulled open the panel to reveal an old-fashioned telephone nestled in a small cupboard.

'Hey,' said a voice inside the box. Charlotte sprang back as the door unlocked and was yanked opened from within. 'Don't do that!'

It was a man in his fifties with a heavily lined face, a crop of grey hair and steel blue eyes.

'Who are you?' Charlotte asked.

'I could ask the same question.' His eyes fell on her camera mounted on its monopod. 'Are you recording me? You're recording me, aren't you?'

His hand went to his jacket pocket, as another voice rang out behind him: younger, female and sort of cockney. 'Who's there, Doctor?'

'You're a doctor?' Charlotte asked. 'Doctor of what?'

The angry man waved the question away. 'A Doctor of ignoring inane questions. Now scram. Vamoose. Do one.'

A girl appeared behind him, pushing the Doctor aside with an affectionate nudge. She had dark skin with expertly shaped eyebrows and hair piled up high on her head.

'Have you heard yourself? "Do one?" Seriously?' She smiled. It was a good smile. A cute smile. She stepped out of the box and pulled up the collar on her shiny silver jacket. 'Nice weather for the time of year.'

'Oh, and what time of year is it, clever-clogs?' the Doctor asked, looking mightily peeved to have been shoved out of the way.

The girl looked up at the sky. 'September?'

'October,' Charlotte corrected her.

She was rewarded by another smile. 'Thanks. I'm Bill, by the way. And you've already met the Doctor.' She leant in conspiratorially. 'Don't worry; he's not always that rude.'

'Yes, I am!' the Doctor argued, shutting the door behind him.

'I'm Cryptogal-UK,' Charlotte told Bill, only to draw a puzzled look from the Doctor.

'What kind of name is that?'

'What kind of name is *Doctor*?'

'A good name. The *best* name.'

Bill grinned. 'Don't tell that to Nigel.' She nodded at Charlotte's phone. 'What are you? Some kind of vlogger?'

Now it was Charlotte's turn to grin. 'Twelve thousand followers and counting!'

'Wow!' Bill looked genuinely impressed. 'What do you do? Gaming and stuff?'

'Gaming?' the Doctor said. 'In a wood?'

Charlotte ignored him. 'Nah, I'm rubbish at games. I hunt monsters.'

'That's a coincidence,' Bill said, pointing at the Doctor. 'So does he!'

Charlotte swung the phone back round to the man. 'You're a vlogger too?' It would explain the name, if nothing else.

'Certainly not,' he replied, peering into the trees. 'Sounds awful.'

'You do know what it means?' Bill asked.

'I'm not that old,' he snapped. 'Video blogging, on YouTube or what have you.' He rummaged in his jacket pocket and pulled out a blue and silver device which whined as he swept it in the air, a green light flashing at its tip.

'What's that?' Charlotte asked.

'None of your business. What kind of monsters do you hunt?'

'The real kind. Bigfoot. Nessie.'

'Which one?'

'What do you mean?'

'Which Nessie do you hunt?'

'There's more than one?'

'I should know. I put them there.'

'What?'

He spun on his heel to face her. 'So you're a Cryptozoologist. Hence the silly name.'

'It's not silly.'

'And a Crypto-whatsit is ...? asked Bill.

'Someone who tracks creatures of myth or legend,' the Doctor explained. 'Life forms conventional science dismisses or ignores. Although most zoologists I know call them "cryptids" rather than "monsters".'

Charlotte shrugged. 'Monsters gets more hits.'

'The question is,' he continued, taking a step towards her, 'what monster are you hunting tonight?'

'There are other questions,' Bill cut in as the Doctor peered at Charlotte with an intensity that made her want to run and hide, video or no video. 'Like where we are?'

'You tell me ...' he replied, as if setting a test.

Bill looked around her. 'Well, I assume we're on Earth, and by the look of that mobile—'

'It's a MeadowPhone 3,' Charlotte told her, a little too eagerly.

'Sweet. They were coming out in August, so it's not far off when we left. Is it still 2017?'

Charlotte frowned. 'Of course it is.'

Bill looked pleased with herself. 'There you go. October 2017.'

The Doctor nodded in appreciation. 'Not bad. As for where we are ...'

'Manchester,' Charlotte offered.

He frowned at her. 'Manchester's a big place. Come on. The devil's in the detail.'

'Huckensall, on the outskirts. Near Sale.'

The Doctor gave her a tight smile. 'See? That wasn't too difficult, was it?'

'Cool,' Bill said, wrapping her arms around herself to keep warm. 'Never been to Manchester.'

The Doctor shook his head, slipping his bizarre buzzing-tool-thing back into his pockets. 'And this is what happens. I show them the stars and they get all giddy about *Manchester*.'

'What's wrong with Manchester?' Bill asked as a scream broke through the trees.

The Doctor was already running in the direction of the cry. 'I suggest we find out. Come on!'

Chapter 6

The Corner of Your Eye

Charlotte suspected that the Doctor was talking to Bill, but followed them anyway.

Someone was crying ahead. A kid, by the sound of it.

The Doctor disappeared down a bank. Bill barely hesitated before following him down the steep incline. Who were these people?

Charlotte started down the slope, slipping almost immediately. She crashed down the hill, landing with a jolt. Groaning, she looked around for her phone. The monopod had slipped from her hand mid-tumble. Where was it?

'Here,' said Bill, retrieving the handset from a pile of leaves and passing it over.

'Thanks.' She checked the screen. It wasn't cracked, thank God.

'You hurt?' Bill asked, helping her up.

Charlotte could feel her face flush, despite the freezing rain. 'Yeah, I'm fine,' she lied, even though her elbow ached from where she had whacked it on her less-than-graceful descent.

'Sorry, is something keeping you two?'

It was the Doctor calling from the bank of a brook that ran between the trees. He was crouching towards a small boy of about 7 or 8, who whimpered as he clutched his ankle. There was a girl too, a couple of years older, doing her best to put herself between him and the kid.

'Leave him alone,' she said defiantly.

The Doctor held up his hands. 'I get it. Don't talk to strange men. I try to do the same, but he's obviously hurt, and I'm a doctor. Just ask my friends.'

Charlotte was shocked that he seemed to include her in that statement.

'It's all right,' Bill told the girl. 'We just want to help. What's your name?'

'Masie,' she replied, still glaring at them both. 'But we're fine, really. I just need to take him home.'

It was clear that the boy was anything but fine. 'They were chasing us,' he snivelled, his words coming out in ragged sobs. 'I fell down the slope.'

The Doctor's glowing stick was out again, waving over the boy's foot. 'Nothing broken,' he concluded. 'Not even a sprain, but that doesn't matter, does it? Because it hurts.'

The boy nodded. 'It really does.'

The Doctor offered a handkerchief covered in question marks to the boy.

'Don't take it,' the girl said.

The Doctor flicked his head towards Masie. 'How old does this one think she is? 27? 45?'

The boy sniffed and smiled. '103.'

'Hey,' Masie complained.

'Older sisters are the worst,' the Doctor said, grinning back at the lad. 'Perhaps I should ban them. I am the President of the World, after all.'

The boy laughed. 'That's silly.'

The Doctor grinned back at him. 'Silly's my middle name. What's yours?'

'My middle name?'

'If you want. Or we could start with your first?'

'Noah,' the boy replied. 'Noah Holland.'

'Good to meet you, Noah Holland.' The Doctor looked up at the girl. 'And big sister Masie too. You don't trust me, do you?'

She shook her head.

'That's fine. Totally fine. But you can trust Bill. That's Bill over there with all the hair. Bill's nice. Nicer than me, anyway. And she's got a question for you, haven't you, Bill?'

Bill crouched down beside Noah and nodded. 'What was chasing you?'

That surprised Charlotte. Bill didn't ask why two kids were out in the middle of the wood, or where they came from. She believed Noah's story without question, and so did the Doctor. The two were tight, like a team. She felt a pang of jealousy.

Noah looked straight at Bill when he answered. 'The Shining Man.'

Charlotte had dropped her smartphone down to her side as soon as they'd found the kids. Now it was up again, trained on Noah. 'What did you say?'

The Doctor stood up and swatted the phone away. 'Point that thing somewhere else. What's wrong with you?'

'No, you don't understand,' she argued. 'That's why I'm here! The Shining Men!'

'And who are they?' Bill asked.

Charlotte snorted. 'You don't know?'

'That's why she asked you,' pointed out the Doctor.

Charlotte couldn't believe it. 'But … everyone knows about them.'

'Bored of talking to you,' the Doctor said, turning his back to her. 'Going to talk to someone who really knows what's going on.' He crouched back down by the children. 'Noah, Masie …. What's a Shining Man?'

Noah shrugged. 'I don't know, they're like ghosts or something.'

'Ghosts?'

'They're these men who appear on street corners, with lights as eyes.'

'I thought they weren't real,' Masie said. 'That's what Mum told me.'

The Doctor nodded. 'Adults have a habit of saying stupid things.'

Masie's face hardened. 'And then one took her away.'

Bill joined the Doctor. 'A Shining Man took away your mum?'

Masie nodded. 'That's what we think. She said she saw one in the street, but never came home.'

'She's been missing for days,' Noah added.

'And then Noah had a dream that wasn't a dream.'

'They're the worst kind,' the Doctor said. 'What happened, Noah?'

Noah's words came out in a burbled rush. 'She needed my help, and was covered in leaves, so we came here to find her and there were lights in the trees, and they chased us through the wood and—'

'And you twisted your ankle,' the Doctor said, calming him. He ruffled the boy's hair, plucking what looked like an acorn from his curls. 'Typical humans. Rushing into danger to help others. No wonder you're my favourite species.'

'What's that mean?' Charlotte asked, but Bill answered with a question of her own.

'So what are they really? These Shining Men?'

Charlotte shrugged. 'That's what I came to find out. This is where it all began.'

'In the wood?' Bill asked, before looking over Charlotte's shoulder. 'What was that?'

Charlotte turned. There was nothing there. 'What was what?'

Bill shook her head. 'The place must be getting to me. I thought I saw something.'

'Out of the corner of your eye?' the Doctor said, standing up again.

'Yeah. It's nothing.'

'Things in the corner of your eye are never nothing. Things in the corner of your eye are usually enough to kill you.'

Bill glanced down at Masie and Noah. 'Doctor, you're scaring the kids.'

'I'm scaring myself.'

She raised her eyebrows. 'Says the man who's never scared!'

'Never is a relative term.' He nodded at the trees behind Charlotte. 'Now, where was it?'

Bill pointed along the bank. 'Over there, beside that tree with the box-thing.'

Charlotte looked at an old elm that the local wildlife trust had used to mount a bird box.

'But I told you,' Bill continued, 'there's nothing—'

Lights appeared behind the tree. Two lights, like eyes.

Charlotte brought up her phone. She wasn't about to miss this, even though her camera seemed to have trouble focusing on the orbs.

'It's him,' Noah snivelled. 'He's come back for us.'

'The Shining Man,' Charlotte said in awe. This was it, what she'd come for. She took a step forward and froze.

She was scared. Really scared, deep in the pit of her stomach. She couldn't move. Couldn't even run. But she wanted to. She really really wanted to.

The eyes blazed in the night, and Charlotte heard a whimper. She thought it was one of the kids and then realised that it was her. Her cheeks were wet, but it had stopped raining. She was crying, her hands shaking, her legs going to jelly. She wanted for the ground to open up beneath her feet, for hands to drag her down into the earth to safety, anything to escape the awful glare of those two piercing eyes.

And then there were more, appearing behind every tree, along the top of the bank, on the other side of the brook. Dozens and dozens of glowing eyes, staring at her. Staring *through* her.

She dropped her phone, sinking to her knees. It felt as though the wood was contracting around her, the air itself pressing in tight, crushing, suffocating.

The Shining Men reached out as one, skeletal fingers searching for her. She rolled into a ball, waiting for their nails to rake against her skin. This had been a mistake. A terrible, stupid mistake, but it didn't matter any more. The Shining Men had come for her.

She was lost.

Chapter 7

Working Undercover

'What is going on here?' said a voice from above.

Charlotte shook her head to clear it. That was a good question. She could move again. The fear and the terror had evaporated, just like that.

She opened her eyes. The lights in the trees were gone as well.

'What are you doing with my grandchildren?' said the voice that had scared the Shining Men away.

'Nanny!' Noah cried out from behind, trying to stand but collapsing in a heap again as his ankle gave way.

'Allow me,' said the Doctor, scampering up the bank to assist the woman who was struggling down towards them. She wore an anorak over her thin nightie, with walking boots on her feet and a woolly hat rammed over grey frizzy hair. The hat was soaked through, but the woman didn't care as she slapped the Doctor's hand away.

'Don't touch me.'

He snatched it back as if burned. 'Suit yourself. I was only trying to help.'

She slithered down the bank, flashlight in hand, and rushed to the children. 'Noah, Masie; what in heaven's name are you doing out here?' She folded her arms around them. 'I was so scared when I found you gone.'

'They chased us, Nan,' Noah told her, resuming his seemingly inexhaustible supply of tears.

The woman shone her flashlight in the Doctor's face like an interrogation lamp. 'They did what?'

'It wasn't us,' the Doctor insisted. 'We heard Noah scream.' He pointed at the boy's leg. 'He's twisted his ankle. It'll be sore for a few days, but nothing that won't mend.'

Charlotte got up and brushed herself down.

Bill sidled up, keeping her voice low. 'You felt that too, right?'

It took Charlotte a moment to realise Bill was talking about the paralysing sense of dread that had accompanied the Shining Men.

The Shining Men! Her footage!

Charlotte snatched her mobile from the ground and checked the display. 'Yes! It recorded!' she said, opening the video app. Rows of eerie eyes stared out of the screen, not quite in focus but better than anything she'd seen online. This was awesome!

'How did you find us?' the Doctor asked, daring to take a step nearer the angry woman.

'What's it got to do with you?'

He tapped the side of his head. 'Inquiring minds need to know.'

The woman looked down at her grandchildren again. 'The man at number fifteen, he told me he saw torches on the playing fields, running towards the trees.' She kissed the top of Masie's head. 'What were you thinking?'

'We were looking for Mum,' the girl replied.

'Oh love. She won't be out here.' She shot a look at the Doctor. 'With these *people*.'

'Who are you calling people?' the Doctor snapped. 'I mean, obviously we're people, but not bad people. We're good people.' He turned to Bill. 'Tell her we're good people.'

'We are,' Bill said, joining him. 'I promise. The Doctor's right; we were just trying to help.'

The old woman's eyes fixed on Charlotte. 'What about that one. I've seen her hanging around the street. You're living out of that camper van, aren't you?'

'I'm with them,' Charlotte said quickly.

'You are?' the Doctor said.

'She is,' Bill told him.

Charlotte realised she that still had her phone up and dropped it down before the old woman could get the wrong idea.

Too late. 'Were you filming us?' The woman started rummaging around in her anorak pocket. 'That's it. I'm calling the police.'

'No need,' the Doctor cut in. 'We're already here. Look.' He fished a battered leather wallet from his jacket and flashed it in front of the woman's face. 'See?' His face fell for a minute, and he glanced at the wallet. 'You do see, don't you?'

'CID?' the woman said, and the Doctor breathed a sigh of relief.

'If that's what it says, then who am I to argue?'

She peered at him with renewed interest. 'You're here about my Sammy?'

The Doctor slipped the wallet back into his coat. 'And that would be Noah's Mum,' he said, obviously bluffing although the woman didn't seem to notice. 'Your daughter.'

'That's right.' She tapped her expansive bosom. 'Hilary Walsh, that's me.'

'Pleased to meet you, Hilary Walsh,' the Doctor replied. 'I'm the Doctor, this is Bill and this ...' He turned to Charlotte and coughed slightly. 'This is Cryptogal-UK, our ... forensic investigator. Hence the inappropriate phone.'

Hilary stared at Charlotte. 'What kind of name is that?'

Before the Doctor could say 'I told you so', Bill cut in: 'It's her code name. For, you know, undercover investigations.'

It was a nice try, but it was clear that Hilary was never going to buy that.

'My name's Sadler,' Charlotte said, stepping forward and held out her hand, trying to look official. 'Charlotte Sadler.'

Hilary glared at the hand as if it was covered in dog muck. 'Well, whoever you all are,' she said, turning back to the Doctor. 'I need to get these two home.' She pulled away from her grandchildren and tutted. 'Coming out here in your pyjamas.'

'You're in your nightie,' the Doctor pointed out, and Bill kicked him in the shin.

'We put our coats on!' Noah told her, wiping his nose.

'You'll catch your deaths.' She shone her flashlight at the lad's ankle. 'Can you walk on it?'

He shook his head. 'I don't think so.' He looked like he was going to start crying again.

'I'll carry him,' the Doctor offered.

'You will?' Bill said.

'Don't sound so surprised,' he berated her.

Hilary looked like she was going to argue, but Noah already had his arms raised, the Doctor hoisting him up into the air. The boy held on tight, giggling as the Doctor made a play of dropping him.

'Careful!' Hilary snapped.

'Don't worry, we'll have him home in no time,' the Doctor said, marching off, before realising that he had no idea where he was going. 'It *is* back this way, isn't it?'

Grabbing Masie's hand, Hilary bustled past him, showing the way with her torch. 'We'll go the long way round. I don't fancy climbing up that bank.'

'Me neither,' the Doctor agreed, following after her. 'What do you feed these kids? He weighs a ton!'

'That's rude!' Noah said, laughing again.

'Don't take it personally. He's like it to everyone,' Bill said, tramping after them, before turning back towards Charlotte. 'You coming?'

Charlotte unclipped her smartphone from the monopod and fell in alongside her. 'Of course,' she said, grinning. 'Where would you two be without your forensic investigator?'

As they walked, Charlotte couldn't shift the idea that they were being watched. She glanced over her shoulder and, just for a moment, thought she saw eyes glowing between the trees, but then they were gone and the wood was dark.

Chapter 8

A Visit from the Doctor

Whether he was a real policeman or not, the Doctor made good use of the walk out of the woods and back across the playing fields. He quizzed Hilary about her daughter's disappearance; how she had slipped out when the kids were in bed and didn't return. Bill chipped in with questions of her own, discovering that Hilary had been staying with her grandchildren ever since their Mum had vanished, and that the police's door-to-door inquiries had been next to useless.

'Don't you know all this, though?' Hilary said, as she bundled Masie through the gate that led onto Brownie Hill.

'Oh, you know what it's like,' the Doctor said quickly, sharing a secret smile with Bill. 'The left hand doesn't know what the right hand's doing.'

'Typical,' Hilary clucked. 'Just like the council. That's how monstrosities like *that* thing happen.'

She jabbed a finger at the building site beside the playing field. Charlotte couldn't see what was wrong with it herself. The house looked like every new build she'd ever seen; a bit on the large side, but nothing out of the ordinary.

Bill seemed to agree. 'Looks OK to me,' she told the old woman. 'Going to be impressive when it's finished.'

'*If* it's finished,' Hilary replied. 'Can't believe they got planning permission. There was nothing wrong with the house that was already there.'

'It was falling down!' Masie said.

'They could have done it up,' Hilary argued, obviously not one to let someone else have the last word. 'At least it had character, not like that eyesore. And the garden ...' Her voice became wistful. 'Sammy loved that garden. Mr Cragside used to let her climb the big tree he had out the back.' She closed the gate behind Charlotte. 'They've pulled that down too. Nothing short of vandalism, if you ask me.'

Charlotte had a feeling that Hilary Walsh would let you know her opinion whether you asked her or not.

Bill at least still seemed interested as Hilary guided them across Brownie Hill and into Bugs Close. 'You've lived here a long time, then?'

'All my life,' she replied, leading them towards a small semi-detached house halfway down the road. A blue Fiat Punto was parked on the paved drive, a row of evergreen shrubs and bushes leading up to the front door. 'This was my place before I moved into the flat. Sammy bought it from me and Ern.'

'Keep it in the family,' the Doctor said, carrying Noah up the path. 'I like that. I had a family home once.'

Hilary looked at him quizzically as she unlocked the door. 'What happened to it?'

'Moved on. Didn't like the neighbours.' He hefted the boy in his arms. 'Where shall I put this?'

Hilary held the door open for him. 'You better take him straight up to his room.'

'Gladly,' the Doctor said. 'Can my squad come too?'

Bill and Charlotte had already stepped into the cosy hallway.

'Doesn't look like I have much choice. I suppose you'll be wanting a cup of tea?'

'If it's no bother,' the Doctor said, grinning as he kicked the door shut for her.

'Well, it *is* late ...'

'We'll just stop for one, then. Seven sugars for me, Bill's sweet enough already. Masie, can you show me to Noah's room?'

The girl led him upstairs, Bill following.

Hilary looked at Charlotte with thinly disguised disapproval. 'And what about you, *Cryptogirl*?'

'I could murder a coffee,' she replied, flashing Hilary her most charming smile. 'Ta!'

She skipped up the stairs to join the others, who were standing in a typical boy's room. There were gaming posters on the wall, action figures crammed into storage boxes and Lego scattered on the floor like a booby-trap just waiting to be stepped on. A desk sat beneath the window in the corner, piled high with comics and magazines, the accompanying chair heaped with crumpled clothes.

The Doctor planted Noah on the bed. 'Nice duvet,' he commented, before helping the lad remove the welly boot from his damaged ankle. The Doctor probed the offending joint before prescribing a course of daydreaming and ice cream. 'You'll be right as rain in no time.'

He spotted a book beside the bed. *The Goblins of Neverness,*' he said, picking it up. 'I haven't read this in years.'

'It's Mum's,' Noah told him. 'She lets me look at it. She's had it since she was a little girl.'

'She likes fairy stories?'

Noah nodded. 'Nan says she always has. I do too.'

The Doctor put the book on the bed and surveyed the messy room. 'Tell me about this dream that wasn't a dream.'

'Mum was standing over there,' Noah said, pointing to the window.

'Covered in leaves and dirt.' The Doctor moved over to the window. 'Which is why you went down to the woods.'

'Noah said she needed our help,' Masie told him.

'And then a Shining Man took her,' Noah said. 'Pulling her down into the floor.'

The Doctor pointed at Masie. 'But you didn't see any of this?'

She shook her head. 'No, but I saw the footprint.'

'And the leaf,' Noah reminded her.

The Doctor grinned. 'A footprint. I love a footprint. Especially a spooky one. It was over here?' He crouched down and ran his fingers over the carpet.

Charlotte peered over his shoulder. 'There's nothing there.'

'But there was,' Masie insisted, pulling away from Bill. Even Noah jumped from the bed and limped over, but Charlotte was right. The carpet was in dire need of a vacuum, but there were no footprints in sight.

'It *was* there,' Masie said, her hands balling into fists by her side. 'It really was. We didn't imagine it.'

'No one said you did,' the Doctor said, sniffing the ends of his fingers before producing his blue and silver gadget again.

'What *is* that?' Charlotte asked.

'The sonic screwdriver,' said Bill as the Doctor ran it over the carpet. 'And before you ask, I don't know what it does either.'

'It helps. Unlike some people,' the Doctor said, returning the screwdriver to his pocket. 'Most of the time, anyway.'

'But not today?' Bill asked.

The Doctor didn't answer. Instead, he bent over and licked the carpet like a cat lapping cream.

'Now what are you doing?' a voice barked from the door. It was Hilary, carrying a tray loaded with steaming mugs.

The Doctor rolled his tongue around his mouth. 'Twenty per cent wool, eighty per cent polypropylene, and a dash of pan-dimensional energy. Interesting.' He jumped to his feet, facing the increasingly outraged grandmother. 'Hilary, you're about to tell us we should leave.'

'I am.'

'Quite right too,' he agreed, walking briskly from the room, only stopping to pluck a mug of tea from the tray.

Hilary stared after him in amazement as he trotted down the stairs, taking an appreciative sip. 'Of all the cheek …' she began as Bill and Charlotte made their excuses and chased after the Doctor.

'I think I like him,' Charlotte as she closed the front door behind them.

'He has that effect on people,' Bill said, looking up at Hilary's scowling face at the window. 'Ninety-nine per cent of the time.'

'That much?' the Doctor said, waiting for them on the pavement, tea still in hand.

'So now what?' Charlotte asked as they joined him.

'Now,' he replied, looking her straight in the eye, 'you tell me everything there is to know about the Shining Men.'

Chapter 9

#fearthelight

Bill liked Charlotte. Not like that. The vlogger was a little too boyish for her underneath that beanie and bomber jacket.

No, it was the way she accepted what was happening, even if that meant putting up with the Doctor. While Bill thought he was all kinds of brilliant, she could see how easily her tutor rubbed people up the wrong way. She had no idea if he did it on purpose, or just didn't realise, but either way Charlotte just went with it. Bill would have to look up her videos when she got home.

The vlogger led them across Bugs Close towards a camper van that had seen better days. Rust eating the battered wheel trims and the chipped yellow paintwork boasted a large collection of dents.

Charlotte slid open the side door. 'Excuse the mess,' she said, beckoning them in. The place almost made Noah's bedroom look tidy. A sleeping bag was scrunched up on a seat that doubled as a bed, the Formica cupboards piled high with plastic plates and bad snacks. The floor wasn't much better, scattered with copies of *Fortean Times* and

Preternatural Monthly, the electric lantern hanging from the low roof offering little illumination.

'Life on the road, eh?' said Bill, clambering into the van.

'I've seen worse,' the Doctor said, depositing himself on the back seat. 'I had a friend who lived in a double-decker bus. She had a thing about leopard-print curtains and dancing hula girls.'

'Sounds great,' said Charlotte, pulling the door shut beside Bill who'd perched on a rickety chair that folded down behind the passenger's seat. 'Velma's a bit of a state, but she keeps me warm at night.'

'Velma?' Bill asked.

'The camper van,' the Doctor guessed, looking around. 'I had a car called Bessie once.'

Bill raised an eyebrow. 'And a TARDIS called Sexy.' She turned to Charlotte. 'He thinks I don't hear him talking to her.'

'What's a TARDIS?' the vlogger asked from where she was crouched on the floor. 'Is that your blue box?'

The Doctor drained his mug and changed the subject. 'Let's see what you've got, shall we?'

Charlotte retrieved a chunky laptop from one of the cupboards and squeezed onto the back seat beside the Doctor. Resting the computer on her knees, she opened the lid, pulling off her beanie hat to reveal tightly cropped hair. The laptop booted up, the light from the screen reflecting against her eyebrow ring.

'OK, the first sighting was a month ago. Since then, Shining Men have been spotted all over the country, usually on street corners, and always looking the same.

Tall and thin, with long dark hair, blank faces and glowing eyes.'

Bill shivered, remember the lights between the trees. 'Like we saw in the woods.'

Charlotte glanced up from the screen. 'I've never seen so many in one place. They're usually alone.'

'And how many have you seen?' asked the Doctor.

The vlogger shifted uncomfortably on the seat beside him. 'Before tonight?'

He nodded.

'OK, I haven't actually seen any at all,' she admitted. 'Not first hand. I've seen photos though, and videos. Lots and lots of videos.' She returned her attention to the laptop, swiping her hand over the touchpad. 'I just need to get online and … there.' She swivelled the laptop around so both of them could see. 'You can always find a Wi-Fi signal if you know where to look.'

A website full of grainy images filled the screen. Each had been taken from a distance and had one thing in common: a tall, shadowy figure just out of focus with a pair of glowing eyes.

'At first it was just in the UK, but there have been sightings in America. Canada too.'

'You said there were videos?' the Doctor prompted.

Charlotte pulled the keyboard back round and checked her bookmarks. 'Here you go.'

A video was already playing when Bill could see the screen again, shaky footage from a mobile phone. It showed an underpass beneath a busy road, the excited chatter of teenagers in the background, before a Shining

Man appeared in the mouth of the tunnel then disappeared again a second later.

'Can I see that again?' the Doctor asked.

'They repeat it,' Charlotte said, as the footage replayed, this time slowed right down so the apparition lingered.

Bill leant in. It was difficult to make out any details except for the luminous eyes which shone like a cat caught in headlights.

'You must have seen these before,' Charlotte said, playing a similar video, a Shining Man appearing beside a motorway this time. 'They've been all over the news.'

'We've been away,' Bill said, leaving the explanation at that.

Charlotte shrugged. 'I thought everyone was talking about it. At first people thought they were just a hoax, some kind of internet prank.'

'But you didn't ...' the Doctor said.

'I knew there had to be something in it. The trouble is that there are idiots out there who've been dressing up as them, scaring kids and the like. It's been difficult to know which sightings are genuine ...'

'And which are people mucking about in costumes,' Bill said.

'Like the ghost impersonators of the nineteenth century,' the Doctor mused, peering at the screen.

'The what?'

He scratched his nose, slipping easily into storytelling mode. 'People think of the Victorians as a rational bunch, with heads full of technology and Empire, but belief in ghosts was so entrenched by the mid-nineteenth century that people *expected* to encounter spooks and spectres wherever they went. It wasn't long before tricksters and conmen took to covering themselves with sheets and jumping out at strangers, specifically women. It looks as though history is repeating itself.'

Charlotte nodded. 'The supermarkets haven't helped. Betterworths has even been selling Shining Men costumes for Halloween, complete with torches for eyes. And then there's Photoshop and Render Plus. Anyone with a half-decent computer can pull off special effects these days. They could all be fake, every single Shining Man video.' She smiled, tapping the pocket where she had stashed her phone. 'Until tonight. This is the proof we've been waiting for.'

'What about the other stuff?' Bill asked.

Charlotte frowned. 'What do you mean?'

'Back in the woods, when all those eyes appeared, I was scared.'

'It's understandable,' the Doctor said. 'You're only human.'

'But I've seen scary stuff before. You know that. This was different.'

'Like you couldn't move,' the Doctor said, flatly. 'Like your body wasn't your own any more.'

'Exactly. I could barely breathe. Like I was trapped.'

'That's in the reports too,' Charlotte told then. 'The ones I think are genuine anyway. An overwhelming sense of claustrophobia.'

'So why here,' the Doctor said, pushing back a flimsy curtain to look out of one of Velma's windows. 'Why Huckensall?'

Charlotte shrugged. 'I told you. This is where it all started.'

'The first sighting.'

She nodded. 'Two months ago.'

'Spreading across the globe in just eight weeks.' The Doctor pointed at the laptop. 'May I?'

'Be my guest,' Charlotte said, handing it over. 'The world's gone Shining Man mad.'

'They even have their own hashtag,' the Doctor said, studying the screen. '#fearthelight. You can tell something's important when it has a hashtag.'

'You know about hashtags?' Bill asked, the thought amusing her more than it should.

The Doctor glared over the top of the laptop. '#insulting. I'm sure you think I live in a box!'

'You kinda do.'

The laptop chimed.

'You've got a message,' the Doctor told Charlotte, peering closer. 'Someone called *MonStar5000*.' His fingers clattered over the keyboard as he typed a reply: '"Hello MonStar500. Congrats on the name. It's nearly as ridiculous as mine …"'

Charlotte snatched the computer from his lap. 'Hey!'

The Doctor sniffed. 'Boring conversation anyway.'

Charlotte's eyes widened as she read the screen. 'No it's not. He's asking if I've seen the live feed on ParaNewsNet.'

'Well, have you?'

'Not yet, but …' She clicked a button.

'Let me see,' Bill said.

Charlotte turned the laptop around to reveal a webcam feed.

'That's a shop,' the Doctor said, sounding singularly unimpressed as Bill made out row upon row of computer hardware boxed on shelves. 'And a closed shop at that. MonStar5000 needs to #get-a-life.'

'That's near here,' Charlotte realised. 'A little computer store in the arcade. I popped in yesterday for an SD card. They must have a webcam running on one of the machines.'

'Why?' the Doctor asked. 'To bore people to death? Because it's working.'

'There,' Bill said, pointing towards the shop window at the back of the grainy image. 'Something moved, on the street outside.'

The Doctor looked closer. 'I don't think so. It's just—'

He jumped back. A face had appeared in the shop window, just for a second. A face with glowing eyes.

'How near is near?' he asked, already making for the door.

'Literally around the corner,' Charlotte answered, reaching for her beanie hat.

The Doctor yanked open the door and jumped out. 'Then what are you waiting for? #move!'

Chapter 10

Gone Shopping

For a man who claimed to be two thousand years old, the Doctor sure could run. He sprinted ahead, his thin legs pumping and booted feet slamming against the pavement.

'Which way?' he shouted, reaching the bottom of Brownie Hill.

'Along the High Street,' Charlotte replied. 'Turn right.'

He took off again. Bill followed without stopping, Charlotte keeping pace beside her. Bill considered for a moment that they must look pretty suspect, two women chasing an old bloke in a velvet suit at midnight, but no one intervened. The road was pretty empty anyway, save for the odd car speeding by, stereo pumping.

'So who are you really?' Charlotte asked as they ran.

'I'm a student,' Bill replied, pleased that she hadn't even broken a sweat. Being with the Doctor was better than a gym membership.

'Where now?' the Doctor called back.

'Left by the Goodfellow,' Charlotte replied.

'The what?'

'The pub,' she said, pointing ahead.

'Got it!' The Doctor ran across the road, Bill glancing both ways before following suit.

'So what is he then? The Doctor?' Charlotte asked, as he disappeared around the corner. 'Your boyfriend?'

That made Bill laugh. 'Not my type, mate. Not by a long shot.'

'Thought so.'

'He's my teacher. He's showing me how the universe ticks, one planet at a time.'

'Like astronomy, you mean?'

'Something like that.'

The Doctor reached the end of the road. This time, Charlotte didn't wait for him to ask.

'Straight over. Alleyway next to Greggs.'

He didn't reply, hurrying across the road.

'You said he hunted monsters.'

'I say a lot of things,' Bill said as they dashed over to the bakery. The Doctor had vanished down a little alleyway between the shops.

'But you've seen this kind of stuff before. Back in the woods, you were scared, but you weren't surprised. Like you expected things to get weird.'

They raced through the walkway, exiting into a little shopping precinct. It was dark until a buzz from the Doctor's screwdriver turned on the street lights one by one. Shops stretched ahead, either side of a row of benches, just what Bill expected from a place like this. Charity shops and discount stores rubbed shoulder with newsagents and a greasy spoon café.

The Doctor was over by a greengrocer, checking a plan of the shopping centre. Bill stopped, catching her breath, but Charlotte wasn't through with the interrogation.

'Are you UNIT?'

Bill looked at her. 'What?'

'You heard. It's either UNIT or Torchwood.' The girl's face visibly paled. 'You're not the Forge, are you?'

Bill raised a hand before she started hyperventilating. 'I honestly don't know what any of that means.'

She jogged over to the Doctor who was busy scraping chewing gum from the plastic map using the end of the sonic screwing.

'Seriously,' he muttered. 'Why do people insist on sticking gum on things. Disgusting habit. It's covering up the shop numbers.'

'Can't you … you know …' She mimicked the sonic and buzzed like a bee.

The Doctor looked appalled. 'It doesn't sound like that.'

'Sorry.'

'Besides the sonic doesn't work on chewing gum. That and wood.'

Bill's eyebrows shot up. 'What kind of screwdriver doesn't work on wood?'

'Don't worry,' said Charlotte, tapping the Doctor on the arm and saving him the embarrassment of a reply. 'I know where it is.'

'At least *someone*'s useful,' the Doctor said, hurrying after the vlogger.

Bill resisted the urge to poke her tongue out at the back of his head.

Charlotte stopped outside a pokey little shop.

'Hardly the Apple Store, is it?' Bill said, taking in the gaudy hand-painted sign. *'PC Planet: for all your computer needs.'*

Charlotte was already filming an establishing shot on her phone. 'It was here, not half an hour ago, that the Shining Man was spotted,' she narrated portentously, turning in a circle.

The Doctor shoved the phone aside before she could get him in shot.

'Hey!' she snapped. 'I'm working here.'

'You're not the only one. Leave me out of it, OK?'

'So, it was standing here,' Bill said, positioning herself where they'd seen the Shining Man on screen. Sure enough, she could see a webcam through the window, a red LED flashing above the lens.

'Excuse me,' the Doctor said, guiding her out of the way.

'Don't mind me!'

'I don't,' he told her, bending down to scan the paving slabs beneath his feet. 'Which is why you're still here.'

She pulled a face. 'Please tell me you're not going to lick the pavement.'

'No need,' he said, standing again. He looked up and down the precinct, Bill following his gaze. To the right were the shops they'd already seen – Poundsaver, the Cats' Protection League and Jean's Café. To the left were Betterworths, Gamez Exchange, and the entrance to a car park.

'How do we feel about splitting up?' the Doctor asked.

Bill shook her head. 'You've never watched a horror movie in your life, have you?'

He looked at her, puzzled.

She raised her hands in front of her, putting on a dramatic voice. 'Our heroes split up, go off alone and are picked off one by one.'

'That never happens,' he insisted. 'Well, hardly ever. Stop being a scaredy-cat.'

'I'm not,' Bill insisted, rubbing her arm as she looked around. 'Shopping centres are just creepy at night, that's all.'

'Clowns are creepy. Shops are just shops.'

Now it was Bill's turn to stare. 'You're scared of clowns?'

'No!' the Doctor said, a little too quickly. 'But can we discuss this later. When we're not standing in the creepy shopping centre.' He pointed back the way they'd come. 'Charlotte, you check back there and I'll have a poke around the car park. Bill can stay here.'

He said it in a way that said she was too scared to look for herself.

'I'll do the car park,' she insisted. 'You never know, Krusty may be hiding behind the shopping trolleys.'

'Ha ha,' he said mirthlessly and checked his watch. 'So, back here in five minutes.'

Charlotte saluted, stopping short of snapping her heels together. 'Aye aye, captain.'

'Be careful,' the Doctor said, waving both of them off before turning his attention back to the pavement outside PC Planet.

Bill chewed her lip as she walked away, the buzzing of the sonic screwdriver a comfort as she crept towards Betterworths.

What was she even supposed to be looking for? This was the Doctor down to a tee; just expecting her to wing it. Probably because he was doing the same. Oh, he liked to pretend he was the man with a plan, but she'd rumbled him almost as soon as they started hanging out. Nine times out of ten, he made it up as he went along.

But he was also right, more often than not. Today was no different. The supermarket ahead of her was just a shop; the aisles dark, the shelves stacked and ready for business. The place would be bustling with OAPs and screaming kids tomorrow. Nothing to be afraid of, unless you got a trolley in the back of your ankles.

She glanced back. The Doctor was scanning the shop window and Charlotte was at the far end of the precinct, recording another video.

Bill peered through the entrance of the car park. The bays were empty, except for a red Volvo parked in the corner and a grimy white van left by the trolleys.

It wasn't even that dark. Strip lighting flickered overhead. The car park only had two floors. How long could it take to have a snoop around? Convincing herself that everything would be fine, she hurried over to the ramp that led to the upper level.

Something flashed up above. She froze at the bottom of the rise, listening for any signs of movement. All was quiet, the Doctor's screwdriver buzzing merrily out in the precinct.

Getting jumpy, she told herself, *that's all*. She started up the ramp. There it was again. A reflection against pipes in the ceiling, two points of light moving across the metal. They were too small for headlamps; too close together for a car.

She stopped where she was, feeling for her mobile in the pocket of her jacket. She pulled it out, scrolling through to the Doctor's number before she realised she had no signal.

Great.

She could go back for him. She *should* go back, but the way he'd gone on about her about being scared … No. She wasn't about to provide him with more ammunition. If he were here, he'd explore, come what may. He would do this, and so could she.

Gripping her phone like a talisman, Bill inched up the ramp, peering over the barrier as she neared the top.

The upper level was just as deserted, a solitary motorbike standing beside a set of swing doors at the far end.

Those must be the stairs, Bill thought as she crept across the empty spaces. Could it have been the bike, a reflection from its lights? She hadn't heard an engine, but touched its black and yellow chassis just to make sure. It was cold, and only had one light anyway.

The payment machine was the only other thing up here, sat in the corner. She glanced at her watch. That had to be five minutes. She'd take the stairs down to the ground floor, anything to get out of here as quickly as possible. She pulled open one of the doors only to recoil. Ugh! The stairs smelled like a urinal. Then there was the strobing fluorescent tubes, straight out of a late-night slasher movie.

'No thanks,' she said, crying out in shock as she turned, bright lights dazzling her. She was pushed back against the door, a gloved hand clamped across her mouth before she could scream.

'Fear the light,' the Shining Man hissed in her ear, its foul breath warm against her cheek.

Chapter 11

PC Schofield

Bill reacted the only way she knew how and brought her knee up hard. She felt the crunch rather than heard it, followed by a sudden grunt. The grip on her arm loosened enough for her to push the Shining Man away.

It stumbled and collapsed to the floor, like a wounded animal. Bill blinked, trying to clear her vision.

'Bill!' came a voice from behind. She moved, just in time to stop herself from being crushed by the door, the Doctor rushing from the stairwell. 'Are you all right?'

Fighting to stop herself from hyperventilating, Bill pointed at the body curled up in a protective ball at their feet. 'Grabbed me ... couldn't see.'

Charlotte crashed through the door. 'Bill? What happened?'

'Our Shining Man,' the Doctor said, his nose wrinkling in disgust as he looked down at the writhing figure. It was wearing a long brown coat, its head covered by glossy black hair. Its eyes were still open, the bright beams of light illuminating nothing but scuff marks and cigarette butts on the floor.

True to form, Charlotte had her phone out, filming the back of its head.

'Let's see if we can get you a better shot,' the Doctor said, reaching down.

The rev of a powerful engine stopped him. Headlights blazed up the ramp, accompanied by a squeal of tyres. With the sudden *whoop* of a siren, a police car accelerated onto the upper level and raced towards them.

The Doctor raised his hands, as if he'd been caught with his fingers in the cookie jar. He was bathed in light as the car screeched to a halt in front of them, Charlotte still filming as they screwed their eyes up against the glare.

The car doors flew open, a female police officer jumping from the driver's seat. She was tall, just shy of six foot, with keen green eyes and blonde hair scraped up into a neat bun beneath her hat. Her partner was even taller, a heavy-set black man who looked like he meant business.

'What's going on here?' the woman demanded.

'My friend was attacked,' the Doctor said, nodding towards the groaning heap of clothes on the floor.

The woman sighed. 'Not another one.'

She nodded at her partner who rolled the Shining Man onto his back. Its face was covered with a black mesh, and Bill could now make out a nose and mouth beneath the fabric. It was a mask, the blazing eyes nothing more than torches set into a domed forehead.

The officer grabbed hold of the cheap polyester wig and pulled, the mask slipping away to reveal a bearded face.

'Up you get,' the policeman said, hauling the man to his feet.

'Let go,' he whined, trying to extract himself from the muscular arm of the law. He pointed an accusatory finger at Bill. 'Sh-she assaulted me!'

'Only after you grabbed me!' Bill spat back.

The female officer turned to the Doctor. 'And you witnessed this?'

'Only the aftermath,' the Doctor replied. 'Police Constable ...?'

'Schofield,' she said, before her eyes fell upon Charlotte. 'And what do *you* think you're doing?'

'Nothing,' Charlotte said, slipping her phone into her back pocket before anyone could take it from her. 'Just, you know, filming evidence.'

'What is it?' Schofield asked. 'Nothing or filming?'

Charlotte flashed her a nervous smile. 'I can email it to you, if you want?'

'We'll see, after you've given us a statement.'

The Doctor's shoulders visibly slumped. 'Must we?'

Bill couldn't believe what she was hearing. 'He jumped me!'

'And paid the price,' the Doctor said, rubbing his hands together as if he was about to stroll away. 'Everyone's happy.'

'I'm not!' the dishevelled Shining Man piped up.

'You're under arrest,' the hulking policeman told him, reading him his rights before shutting him in the car.

'Bravo,' the Doctor cheered, piloting Bill and Charlotte towards the stairs. 'Justice is served. You've got your man, so I guess we'll be off.'

'Then you guess wrong,' Schofield said, stepping in front of them. 'What were the three of you doing here?'

The Doctor nodded in the direction of the shops. 'Bargain hunting.'

'Is that right?'

'Probably.'

'Do we need to arrest you as well?' Schofield's partner said, crossing his arms across an imposing chest.

'No,' Bill said, stepping forward. 'We were looking for him, OK?' She nodded at the creep in the back of the car. 'Well, not him exactly, but …'

'But a Shining Man,' Schofield said, the frustration evident in her voice.

'We saw him on a webcam,' Charlotte cut in. 'It's all over the net.'

Schofield looked them up and down. 'So you came looking for monsters.' She fixed the Doctor with a glare. 'Aren't you a little old to be hanging around with these two?'

'More than you know. But tell me, what did you mean by "another one"?'

'Sorry?'

'"Not another one." That's what you said. This is becoming a problem, yes? People dressing up.'

'That's an understatement.'

'Around the shops. Near Noah Holland's school.'

That got Schofield's attention. 'What do you know about Noah Holland?'

The Doctor flicked open his psychic paper. 'Doctor John Smith. UNIT.'

'I knew it!' Charlotte hissed behind him, only to be silenced by a look from Bill.

'Am I supposed to be impressed?' Schofield said, although her jaw had clenched the moment the Doctor had made his claim.

'You know what UNIT is?'

'I've heard rumours.'

The Doctor returned the wallet to his pocket. 'Then you should listen to them.'

Bill tried her best to keep her expression neutral, but couldn't help but be surprised. She'd never heard the Doctor speak like this. She knew he had his secrets – his mysterious vault back at the university, for one – but this didn't sound like him. What – or who – was UNIT?

Whatever the word meant, it had the desired effect. Schofield's lips thinned to an angry line, but her attitude became one of grudging compliance. 'It's getting out of control. We've arrested three jokers in the past week alone, all in the same get-up, all out to cause trouble. Hanging around schools, in alleyways—'

'In car parks?' the Doctor offered.

'But what's the point?' Bill asked. 'It's the middle of the night. No one's here.'

'You are,' Schofield countered. 'You saw him on a webcam and came running. Exactly what he wanted. As for the others, maybe it's a cry for help, maybe they're just doing it for kicks.'

'Could be a protest,' Charlotte cut in.

'Against what?' Bill asked.

Charlotte shrugged. 'Law and order? The Nanny State? Giving all those CCTV cameras something to look at?'

'Whatever it is,' Schofield said, talking over her, 'we're the ones who have to clear up the mess.'

'What mess?' the Doctor asked.

Schofield sighed. 'Yesterday, a bunch of kids saw a Shining Man hanging around in Stamford Park. You know what kids are like – they exaggerated, the story grew. Before long they were telling everyone that the Shining Man had a baseball bat and had tried to shove one of the lads into a sack. It gets back to one of the dads. He rounds up his mates and heads down to the park. They find the guy, they put him in hospital, all because he decided to put a costume on one morning. He was lucky; he got away with three broken ribs and a punctured lung.'

'Doesn't sound lucky to me,' Bill said.

'It could've been worse,' the Doctor commented.

'Much worse,' Schofield agreed. 'How long before one of these idiots jump out at someone with a heart condition? Or a victim fights back, that little bit too hard?' Schofield glanced pointedly at Bill. 'The papers don't help, blowing everything out of proportion. People are scared around here.'

'And not just here,' the Doctor said. 'All over the country.'

'Exactly. Now, are you going to give me a statement, or do we have to discuss this at the station?'

Bill stepped forward before the Doctor could answer. 'Sure. No worries. What do you need to know?'

Half an hour later, Bill had explained what happened and given her home address and mobile number.

Realising that she wasn't going to get much further with the Doctor, Schofield told her colleague to get back in the car. Before she joined him, she turned back to the Doctor. 'Remember what we said. It's only a matter of time before someone gets hurt.'

He nodded. 'I promise. That's the last thing I want.'

Schofield didn't look convinced as she opened the car door. Then she stopped, noticing Charlotte's mobile held surreptitiously in her hand.

'Are you still filming? Exactly what evidence are you collecting?'

The Doctor stepped between them, blocking Charlotte's shot. 'She's not collecting anything. Probably taking a selfie. You know what young people are like. It's all about them, them, them.'

The police officer looked as if she was going to retaliate, before giving up. She slipped back into the car, slammed the door and drove off, their prisoner scowling from the back window. The Doctor gave a friendly wave as the police car disappeared down the ramp and they were alone again. No police. No Shining Man. Just Bill, Charlotte … and the Doctor's bad mood.

'Seriously?' he said, turning on Charlotte. 'You were filming her for your vlog?'

Charlotte sniffed, trying to look nonchalant. 'It's a free country.'

The Doctor pointed a bony finger at her mobile. 'That phone will be the death of you.'

'Melodramatic, much?' Charlotte scoffed, shoving the handset into her pocket, but the Doctor wasn't listening. He had turned to Bill, resting a hand on her shoulder.

'Are you all right?' he asked, his voice as gentle now as it had been furious a moment before.

Now it was Bill's turn to act as though she wasn't bothered, even though he could probably feel that she was still shaking. 'Yeah, course I am. I can look after myself.'

'You shouldn't have to. I'm sorry. I should never have suggested splitting up. It was stupid of me. It's just been a while since I've done this.'

'Done what?'

Sadness filled his ageless eyes. 'Had a friend. I'm out of practice.'

'What about Nardole?' Bill asked. Nardole was the Doctor's factotum back at the university, a funny little man in every sense of the word. Bill hadn't quite worked him out yet, from the strange things he said to the nuts and bolts she kept finding wherever he'd been.

The Doctor gave a half-smile. 'Nardole's a special case.'

She grinned. 'Ain't that the truth.' She leant closer, dropping her voice as if imparting a great secret. 'And don't worry, you're doing fine with the friend thing.'

'Shhh,' he whispered back. 'Don't tell anyone. I have a reputation to protect.' Then, without warning that he was about to change tack, the Doctor held out his hand to Charlotte. 'Give it here.'

'You what?'

'Your phone. You'll want to give it to me.'

'I don't think so!'

'Oh, you don't think so.' He produced his sonic, waving it in front of his face. 'And there was me thinking you wanted to produce a killer video.'

She narrowed her eyes. 'What are you talking about?'

'I have data on here that will blow your socks off.'

Now they went wide. '*UNIT* data?'

'Not here!' he hissed, looking around. 'Walls have ears.' His hand went out again. 'May I?'

Without hesitation this time, Charlotte pulled out her phone and handed it to him.

'Thanks for trusting me,' the Doctor said, firing the sonic at the mobile. The handset beeped and he passed it back. 'Now, don't look at that until you're safely back in Velma.'

Charlotte's thumb hovered above her touchscreen. 'Why?'

The Doctor tapped the side of his nose. 'Ask no questions, get told no lies. But, it'll be worth it, just you wait and see.'

She beamed, slipping the phone back into her pocket. 'So what about you two?' She looked at Bill, a little too hopefully. 'Do you need somewhere to crash?'

The Doctor answered for her. 'We have the TARDIS.'

Bill smiled as Charlotte tried to hide her disappointment. 'Your blue box?'

He was already walking towards the stairs. 'Our home away from home. Come on, Bill.'

'So what's UNIT?' asked Bill as they trudged back through Boggle Wood.

'Useful when I want it to be,' the Doctor replied, searching through his pockets for the TARDIS key. 'But one thing at a time. It's getting late.'

'*Getting* late? It must be two o'clock in the morning?' Bill said, glancing at her watch, not that it would do her any good. Time zones got hazy when you travelled by TARDIS.

'Exactly,' he said, as the police box came into view. 'We need to be up and at 'em in the morning. Fresh as a daisy!'

Bill had never been so glad to see anything in her life. Their walk through the woods had been free of incident, but she couldn't shake the feeling that eyes were crawling all over her from the shadows. Still, she couldn't believe the Doctor was calling it a night.

'How can you sleep with all this going on?' she asked as he opened the door and disappeared inside.

'Who's sleeping?' he shot back, marching over to the console and getting busy with the controls. 'Shut the door, will you?'

Bill did as she was asked, joining him at the ship's controls.

'No, sleep is for tortoises.' The Doctor finished his calculations and slammed down the dematerialisation lever. 'Besides, we're taking a short cut.'

A pair of glowing eyes watched as the TARDIS faded away to nothing. The wood was silent again, save for the sound of sobbing in the darkness.

Chapter 12

In for Christmas

The last person Rob Hawker wanted to see was Harold-blooming-Marter. It was bad enough that the boys were expected to work on a Saturday, without the owner appearing unannounced at the building site to stick his oar in.

Just the sight of him put Rob's back up. Marter had perfect clothes, perfect hair and perfect teeth, none of which stopped him being a perfect pain in the backside.

'Well,' Marter said, stomping into the house, 'what have you got to say for yourself?'

There was a lot Rob wanted to say. That they should be left to get on with their jobs. That the build wouldn't be so far behind schedule if Marter didn't keep changing his mind. That he could stick his new house where the sun didn't shine.

But telling the man who paid the invoices where to go was never a clever idea, so Rob bit his tongue and told him that everything was going all right instead.

Matter looked at the foreman as if he was dirt, and particularly stupid dirt at that. 'Is that what you call it?

None of the windows are in and most of the rooms are still missing floorboards!'

'We'll get it done,' Rob promised, willing to say anything if Marter would leave. The firm's builders mate, Tim, would be back with the bacon butties any minute. Rob wanted to eat his breakfast in peace.

'That's what you said last week,' Marter reminded him.

'And we're getting there. I had two men off with the flu last week—'

'Not my problem,' Marter interrupted.

'But they're back on the job now,' Rob continued, gritting his teeth. 'So we'll make up the time, no worries.'

'You'd better. The electrician is coming in on Monday.'

'I know. I booked him.'

'And the plasterer needs to get started by the end of the week.'

Rob forced himself to nod. It was either that or throttle the jumped-up little prat. 'Trust me. The guys know what they're doing.'

'I promised Kate that we'll be in for Christmas.'

'And you will be,' Rob assured him, imagining Christmas in the Marter household. Dinner parties with their posh mates, comparing log burners and holidays in the south of France. The Christmas tree would be pristine, of course, with colour-coded baubles carefully aligned. She'd probably already bought the decorations, ready to impress the new neighbours.

Rob had nothing against people with money. Why would he? People with money wanted large houses, and as long as Rob was the one building them, then everyone was happy. Everyone except idiots like Marter who thought that money in the bank was a licence to throw your weight around. He doubted Marter had ever done a proper day's graft in his life. Pushing numbers around a computer before rushing to the gym to work off the carbs; what kind of life was that? Marter had it all. The looks, the cash, the soon-to-be-completed dream house, and yet the bloke never even cracked a smile.

At least he'd stopped arguing. 'OK, if you say so.'

'I do,' Rob reassured him, putting on his best get-the-customer-out-the-door smile. 'We'll be back on track in no time. You'll see.'

Marter didn't look convinced, but turned to leave all the same, and just in time too. Tim was back from the café, swinging a plastic bag and whistling tunelessly.

'Laters then,' Rob said, cheerfully.

But Marter stopped at the door, fishing his phone out of his pocket. 'There was just one more thing.'

Rob's shoulders sagged. Of *course* there was.

Marter flicked through pictures on his screen. This was a bad sign. Pictures meant that Mrs Marter had spotted something in a magazine that she just had to have, no matter what the cost, or the delay to the project.

Sure enough, Marter walked back to him. 'Kate wanted me to ask you about the patio doors.'

Oh no. Not that. Harold's missus had changed her mind about them three times already.

'They're going in this morning,' Rob told him.

'Then you'd better let me see,' Marter said, striding through to the room that would eventually be his living room.

'Wait! You need a hard hat!' Rob turned to Tim. 'Chuck us one over, will you?'

Tim grabbed a yellow helmet from a pile near the front entrance and threw it across the hall.

'Thanks,' Rob said, catching it. 'I'd hate for something to fall on his head.'

'Yeah,' the lad sniggered. 'Nightmare.'

There was a flash of light from the living room. Marter must be taking photos.

'Seriously though,' Rob said, following the owner into the bare room, 'if you want the wiring done on Monday …'

He trailed off. The lounge was empty. He peered out of the hole that had been left for the patio doors. Outside was a muddy patch of land that would one day be transformed into a beautiful garden.

Marter wasn't out there either.

'Mr Marter?' Rob said, walking back into the hall, and checking in the similarly empty kitchen. 'Harold?'

There was no sign of the man.

'Where'd he go?' he asked Tim.

The crater-faced lad shrugged and produced a sandwich from his plastic bag. 'Did you want red or brown sauce?'

Chapter 13

Lore of the Land

Bill had heard of breaking into houses, she'd heard of breaking into banks, but she'd never heard of anyone breaking into a public library.

As if she needed more proof that the Doctor wasn't just anyone.

'Are you *absolutely* sure this is a good idea?' she asked, looking furtively over her shoulder. The high street was quiet, most of the shops still shut, but cars were already passing back and forth, a single-decker bus trundling by.

'Of course it is,' the Doctor insisted, unlocking the door with the sonic screwdriver. 'When have I ever have a bad idea?' He bundled her in before she could answer, locking the door behind them.

'Just tell me that you're not going to steal any books!'

'What do you take me for?'

'The man who tried nick a diamond on Saturn?' she said, remembering their recent visit to the far future.

'That was different,' the Doctor said, disappearing between the stacks.

'Then what are we looking for?' she called after him.

'Books and stuff.'

'What kind of stuff?'

'Interesting stuff. Useful stuff.'

'Yeah, that narrows it down …'

She looked up at the clock above the librarian's desk. Quarter to nine. Bill removed her watch and twisted the dial.

'What are you doing?' the Doctor said, poking his head over a bookcase.

'Setting my watch to local time,' she said, slipping it back on her wrist. 'First rule of travel.'

'That's the second rule,' he told her, vanishing again. 'The first rule is never forget the Wirrn repellent.'

'Either way, we haven't got long,' she said, finding him with his nose in a copy of *A Bear Called Paddington*. 'The library opens at ten.'

He slipped the book back into a rack. 'How do you know that?'

'The sign on the door. The last thing we need is an angry librarian.'

'Nonsense,' he said, running his fingers along the spines of the shelves. 'Librarians love me. Except for that lot in Alexandria, but the fire wasn't my fault. Ish.' He stopped, pulling a heavy black tome from the shelf. 'Here we are. Hold your arms out.'

'Why?'

He start piling book after book into her hands. 'Because you need to hold this, and this, and this, and this!'

'Er, heavy …' she complained, nearly dropped the steadily growing pile.

'Sorry, allow me,' he said, plucking the thinnest possible pamphlet from the top of the stack and rushing over to a reading table. 'Well, come on, we haven't got all day.'

Bill slammed the books down, the pile immediately toppling over.

'Careful,' he said, stopping the books from crashing down on the cup of tea that had appeared on the table. She had a sneaking suspicion that the Doctor had produced the cup from his jacket pocket, complete with a shortcake biscuit, but knew better than to ask too many questions.

'Where's mine, then?' she asked.

'What?'

She pointed at the china cup.

'Oh sorry,' he said, sliding it over to her. 'Please, have this one.'

She wasn't going to argue, although she couldn't help but notice that the biscuit had disappeared from the saucer. 'So, what do we need?' she asked, taking a sip and wincing at the amount of sugar.

'I'll know when we find it,' he said unhelpfully, brushing crumbs from his lapel. He shoved a hardback book towards her.

Bill picked it up, reading the name on the spine. '*Lore of the Land* by Amelia Rumford.' She opened it at random, finding a chapter on standing stones. 'Haven't you got a library on the TARDIS?'

'It's out of bounds at the moment,' the Doctor admitted, as he flicked through a book of his own. 'The books are possessed.'

Bill actually laughed at that. 'They're what?'

'Possessed,' he repeated as if such things happened every day. 'Last time I went in there, poor Hattie got attacked by the 1986 *Bash Street Kids* annual. It had grown teeth the size of bananas.' Bill was just about to ask who Hattie was when the Doctor slapped the page he was reading. 'A-ha!'

'A-ha what?'

He flashed the cover of the book at her. '*The Encyclopaedia of British Myth and Legend*, seventh edition. B for Boggart.'

'That bloke from old movies?'

The Doctor looked up at her. 'Sorry?'

Bill put on an American accent that admittedly needed work. 'Play it again, Sam.'

He sighed. 'Not Bogart … Boggart. Listen …' He returned to the page, reading out loud. '"A mischievous goblin or sprite most notably associated with the counties of Lancashire and Yorkshire".'

'Oh yeah,' Bill remembered. 'There's one in Harry Potter.'

He shot her a grin. 'You wait to see what happens in book ten. Ron and Hermione have to find an Occamy's scale and …'

'Doctor …'

'Oh yes, sorry. So, Boggarts were the original Bogey-Men, or Bugges.'

'Bugs Close!' Bill realised.

He nodded, running his finger along the page as he read. '"Other names for the creature includes Bo-ghasts, Bogill-boos and Boggles."'

'As in Boggle Wood.'

'The very same. According to this, they're why you shout "Boo" if you're trying to scare someone.'

'What did they look like?'

The Doctor scanned the page. 'It doesn't say. What about Amelia?'

'Who?' she asked.

He nodded at the book.

'Oh.' Bill checked the index, finding an entry on Boggarts. She flicked to the page and her eyebrows shot up.

'What is it?' asked the Doctor.

She turned the book around so that he could see. There was an illustration of a Boggart, tall and lanky, with swinging arms, long clumpy hair and eyes that burned like torches. 'Look familiar?' she asked.

Chapter 14

Ultra-Terrestrials

Bill flicked through the book finding one gruesome illustration after another. 'But, Doctor,' she began. 'Goblins …'

The Doctor let out a groan. 'You're not going to come over all Scully on me, are you?'

She screwed up her nose. 'You what?'

He lapsed into a cockney accent that would make Dick Van Dyke wince: '"But, Doc*tah*, *gobberlins* aren't real, are they me old china?"'

'Is that supposed to be me?'

'I don't know,' he replied brusquely, pushing his chair away from the table. 'I thought you had an open mind.'

'I did. I mean, I do,' she said, standing up herself.

The Doctor had rushed over to a bank of computers next to the local history section. He blasted one of the monitors with the sonic, frowning when the screen refused to turn on.

Bill leant across and pressed the power button. 'It's a lot to take in, that's all. You know … fairies.'

'It's not that hard to believe, is it?' he said, as the computer booted up. 'I mean, I had trouble believing in humans when I was a Time Tot, and yet here you are.'

She sat down, as the Doctor opened a web browser. 'That's not exactly the same.'

'Isn't it?' he said, swivelling to face her. 'You exist, they exist.'

'What, like Tinkerbell?'

'If she has green skin, razor-sharp teeth, and the unfortunate habit of stuffing rose petals down her victims' throats, then yes, they're exactly like Tinkerbell.'

'So, they're alien?'

He was typing into the search bar now. 'Not every horror comes from the stars. Fairies are from Earth, and have around just as long as humans, maybe even longer. Remind me to ask Vastra if they were around in her day.'

Bill had no idea who that was, but didn't want the Doctor to get distracted again. 'But wouldn't we notice if there were fairies flapping around everywhere?'

'Who says you don't? History's full of sightings.' He started clicking through his search results. 'There.' He opened a newspaper report from the *Manchester Evening News*, dated 2 April 2014. 'The Rossendale Fairies,' he said, indicating a picture that showed blurry creatures flying in front of greenery. Each had a tiny set of wings. 'A lecturer from Manchester Metropolitan took this when out walking.'

'I saw this on the news,' Bill said. 'They said they were midges or something.'

'Well, they would, wouldn't they, whoever *they* are. It's easier to believe than the alternative.'

'That they're real.'

His chair creaked as he leant back. 'They've had more names than I've had faces. Fairies. The Fae. The Fair Folk. *Homo fata vulgaris …*'

Bill held up a hand to stop the list. 'I get the idea.'

He started flicking through the sites he'd pulled up, revealing photos and paintings, cartoons and sketches. 'They're ultra-terrestrials; beings who live alongside humans, but out of sight. In the Invisible.'

'And what's that?'

'Earth but not Earth. Think of it as a different frequency, that most humans can't perceive.'

'Like dogs and whistles.'

He nodded. 'They evolved here on Earth, but have an interesting relationship with the laws of physics, doing things that shouldn't exactly be possible.'

'So, they're magic?'

'No. There's no such thing as magic. Just different rules.'

'You said the TARDIS was magic, when I first came on board.'

'I said the TARDIS was science *beyond* magic. There's a difference.'

Bill watched as he continued scrolling through the pictures.

'And these ultra-terrestrials, they can be anywhere, and we can't see them.'

'Yes.'

She shivered. 'That's not creepy at all.'

'Oh, it is,' the Doctor said. 'It's even worse than clowns.' He pointed past her. 'There's one, behind you, by the way. Right now.'

She jumped, spinning around, but there was nothing there. 'That's not funny,' she told him.

That didn't stop him grinning. 'No, but it's how it works. Back when the world was younger, the veil between the Invisible and the Visible was thinner. Ultra-terrestrials could pass back and forth whenever they wanted. Our friendly neighbourhood fairies, well, they caused merry hell. People saw them. People were afraid of them – and for good reason. To them, we're just playthings.'

'But what changed? Why don't people see them any more?'

'Oh, you do.'

'Me?'

'You just don't realise. A half-glimpsed movement. The shadow in a corridor that looks almost human. Voices shouting in the dark when there's no one there. Ghosts ... UFOs ... Why do you think people talk about little green men?' He turned back to his computer screen. 'Of course, there aren't as many as there used to be. The Fae aren't very good with straight lines and buildings. They prefer natural spaces and woodlands.'

'Like Boggle Woods.'

The Doctor had spied a book on a nearby shelf. He wheeled over and grabbed it. 'Local history,' he said, flicking through the pages as he returned to the computer. There was a map at the front of the book, a hamlet by a wood. 'Huckensall village, long before it was swallowed up by the city.' He flipped on a couple of pages, finding a paragraph that interested him. 'Most of the doors in the village were made from wood from the rowan tree. Interesting.'

'Why?'

'Because traditionally rowan trees were used for protection against fairies. It was the custom to carry rowan crosses in your pocket, bound with red twine. The berries even have a five-pointed star opposite their stalks.' He brought up a picture on the screen.

'It's like a pentagram,' Bill said.

'It *is* a pentagram, the Doctor confirmed. 'While ultra-terrestrials draw energy from nature, there's something about rowan that forms a natural defence. They can't pass through it as they can other woods.'

'Hence the doors.'

The Doctor found another passage in his book. 'Here we go: "According to legend, Huckensall was a hotbed for Boggarts and goblins for hundreds of years. They invaded people's homes at night; snatching sheets from beds with invisible claws, and knocking objects from shelves …"'

'"There were even reports of unnatural storms and gales *inside* the huts and cottages,"' Bill read, looking over his shoulder, '"the Church of St Bartholomew-in-the-Mead suffering a torrential hailstorm *within* its walls on a day when there wasn't a cloud in the sky."'

The Doctor looked grave. 'They must have lowered their psionic defences.'

'Is that what attacked the TARDIS? A Boggart?'

'Maybe that's what we saw in the wood.'

'But what did the villagers do?' Bill asked. 'Back then?'

The Doctor checked the book. 'There's a report from 1654. A Fairy Finder came to the village.'

'Is that good or bad?'

'Depends on who you are. Fairy Finders were the pest controllers of their day. They rounded up the Fae and buried them deep in the ground.'

'Did it work?'

He looked up at her, not getting her meaning.

'The Fairy Finder. Did he see off the Boggarts?'

'It doesn't say.' Putting the book aside, he returned to the computer, pointing at the screen in front of Bill. 'Charlotte said that the first Shining Man sighting was made around here. See what you can find. Newspaper reports. Interviews.' He glanced over his shoulder at the clock. 'And make it snappy. I don't want to put my theory about librarians to the test.'

Bill got to work, firing up the computer and beginning her search.

Shining Men Huckensall

She hit return and was surprised to see Charlotte's face pop up, smiling from a video thumbnail. She followed the link to YouTube and her heart sank as she read the description.

'Er, Doctor ...'

He turned, spotting Charlotte. 'Ah, speak of the devil. Well, what are you waiting for? Press play.'

He's not going to like this, she thought, sitting back to watch the fireworks.

Charlotte appeared on screen, walking along Bugs Close, talking straight to camera.

'Hey guys. I'm here in Huckensall, near Manchester, where the entire Shining Man phenomenon began. Yesterday, I saw a Shining Man. In fact, I saw loads. Not one, not two, but a whole pack of them, near here in Boggle Woods.'

'She's good,' commented the Doctor. 'The camera likes her.'

Bill closed her eyes, waiting for the inevitable.

Charlotte continued, becoming more animated: 'And I got it on camera. All of it. The woods. The Shining Men. Even eye witnesses that could corroborate my story.'

A grin crept over the Doctor's face.

'But then I lost it. All the footage. It was gone, wiped by someone I trusted. Someone who said he would help.'

Bill's eyebrows shot up. 'Doctor, you didn't?'

'Didn't what?'

'Don't come the innocent with me. You wiped her phone. In the car park. When you said you were giving her files.'

He tried to look innocent. 'Who? Me?'

Bill paused the video. 'Why would you do that? Why destroy her stuff?'

Now he looked serious. 'Why? Because ultra-terrestrials like the Boggarts thrive on fear. Strong emotions weaken the veil between the Visible and the Invisible. They can use them to jump from their world to ours. You heard PC Schofield. People are already scared, and a video of what we saw in woods? That would go viral in seconds, spreading the terror view by view, like by like. The more people that are scared, the easier it'll be for Boggarts to attack.'

'And that's what they're doing? Attacking?'

The Doctor started counting off on his fingers. 'People disappearing. Strange apparitions. Unnatural storms. Sounds like an attack to me. Don't you see, Bill? I had to stop her.'

She shifted uncomfortably in her chair and bit her lip. 'I don't think you did.'

The Doctor's face fell. 'What do you mean?'

Bill restarted the video, Charlotte springing back to life. '*He didn't want anyone to see my footage, to see the truth.*' A smile spread across her lips. '*But that doesn't matter, because the truth has a way of coming out.*'

The picture cut to grainy night-vision footage: Boggle Woods captured in green and black. Charlotte was running through the trees, towards a familiar groaning sound, like the universe being torn apart.

She zoomed in on a police box standing in the middle of a clearing, its windows bright against the gloom.

'But that's impossible ...' the Doctor muttered.

'*He wiped my phone,*' Charlotte continued, talking over footage of her trying to open the TARDIS door. '*But everything I shoot automatically backs up to the cloud. Including his face.*'

The door pulled open and the image froze on the Doctor's face as he looked angrily from his box.

'*This is the Doctor,*' Charlotte said. '*And if you want to see what he tried to destroy, then like this video and I'll post the footage tomorrow.*'

'No!' the Doctor said, jumping up from his seat. 'She can't.'

'She kinda already has.'

'She put me online,' the Doctor spluttered. 'Nobody puts me online.' He pulled out the sonic and blitzed the computers.

'Now what are you doing?' Bill asked.

'Wiping the browser history. We need to stop her.'

He made for the doors, just as they were unlocked by a startled lady in thick coat.

'W-who are you?' she stammered. 'What were you doing in there?'

The Doctor put a finger to his lips and shushed her before running out into the street. 'Keep your voice down. This is a library!'

Chapter 15

Levelling up

Charlotte's smartphone buzzed, a notification flashing across the screen.

'*Congratulations! Your video has been watched 8,000 times. Keep going.*'

Don't worry, I will, Charlotte thought, popping open a tube of cheese and chive Pringles to celebrate. The breakfast of champions.

She glanced up at her laptop screen, perched on top of Velma's cupboards. Another 400 people had viewed the video in the last minute alone. This was it! Cryptogal-UK was officially going viral, and it was all thanks to the Doctor.

She smiled as she imagined his face when he saw the video. That would teach him. You can't go round wiping people's phones, whether you're UNIT or not.

Still, she'd had the last laugh.

Comments were appearing beneath the video now, including some of the biggest cryptozoologists in the trade, names she'd admired for years. They were heaping praise on the video, asking questions and – most importantly – theorising what she had in store for her next vlog.

Suddenly everything that happened over the last twenty-four hours was worth it. Getting soaked in the woods. Getting scared senseless. Today was the day when Cryptogal-UK levelled up. Today was when people took her seriously.

Well, most of them.

A new comment appeared, with an all-too-familiar name.

YetiHunter1997.

The guy was a jerk. Everyone knew it. But they also listened to what he had to say, even if it was mainly trolling. She'd met him once, at a convention, and he couldn't have been more different to his online persona. In person, YetiHunter1997 was an ineffectual douche who could barely maintain eye contact.

Huddled safely in his bedroom, the mouse of a man became a monster. Armed with an ergonomic keyboard and a complete lack of self-awareness, YetiHunter1997 was never happier than when pummelling others into submission with one of his many, many opinions.

This morning was no different. Crunching another mouthful of crisps, Charlotte scrolled down.

New Comment: @YetiHunter1997 – 27 seconds ago

Huh. Obviously fake. She's got nothing and she nos it. Better luck nxt time girlie. #Lame

The hashtag was followed by a line of smug emoticons that rolled back and forth in mocking hysterics.

'Ignore him,' Charlotte said out loud. 'He's not worth it.' But even as she said it, she knew she couldn't let him have the last word.

She snatched the laptop from the cupboard, already composing a reply that would make his ego bleed. Smiling to herself, Charlotte started typing.

Hey neckbeard, why don't you do us all a favour an

'No!' Charlotte's cursor was replaced by the spinning ball of doom.

She clicked on the Wi-Fi icon. The signal had completely vanished. In fact, *all* the networks in Bugs Close had disappeared, both secure and insecure. Had there been a power cut?

She reached over to the window to pull back the curtain and the van rocked.

'Hey!'

It happened again, harder this time. She jumped out of the seat, her computer slipping from her lap to crash to the floor. She swore, throwing out a hand to steady herself. Velma swayed back and forth, her suspension creaking. Someone was outside. For a moment, Charlotte had the crazy thought that it was the loser that had attacked Bill, but he'd still be locked up, wouldn't he?

The rocking got worse. She fell forward, landing beside her laptop. 'Cut it out! What do you think you're doing?'

The door rattled, but the lock held. She yanked at the curtain to see who was outside and screamed, stepping back, the laptop screen crunching beneath her foot.

The curtain had fallen back, but the face she'd seen lingered in her mind. The snarling mouth. The crooked nose. The burning eyes.

It had to be a mask. Yeah, that's what it was. Kids trying to scare her.

Congratulations. Mission accomplished.

Her phone bounced down from the cupboard. She snatched it up, trying to call 999.

No reception. Damn it!

She was thrown against the cupboard, the thin wood splintering against her weight. 'Stop it,' she yelled, not expecting an answer.

She got one anyway. Rasping voices, like nothing she had ever heard.

'Where is the Lost? Where?'

Something was scraping against the outside of the van, the windows, the doors. She wanted to believe it was keys, but knew that it wasn't.

She held her phone up with shaking hands. She may not be able to call for help, but she could record what was happening. She tapped the camera app, and a blue spark erupted from the screen. She yelped in surprise, throwing the handset across the van.

Velma bounced, as if she was being lifted from the ground and dropped again. They were going to turn her over. Charlotte curled into a ball, screwing her eyes up tight, as the world went mad. The cracked screen of her laptop flared before dying completely, smoke rising from the keyboard. Static burst from the speakers in the door, the radio turning itself on to blare nothing but white noise.

And then a blinding flash of light burned through the windows, turning her eyelids red.

Charlotte's own scream joined the wail of the speakers before they stopped dead. Everything stopped. The sibilant voices from outside. The scrape of nails against metal. Even the rocking. The only sound in the van was the rasp of her own frightened breath.

Charlotte opened her eyes and looked around. Light was streaming through the thin curtains, but it was wrong. It took a moment to realise why.

The light wasn't the dull grey of a damp October morning. It was warm and bright, like a summer's day. She listened, still wrapped in a ball. There was no traffic, the constant thrum of cars and lorries in the next road gone. Instead, Charlotte could hear the twittering of a thousand birds. That wasn't an exaggeration. She had never heard so many birds, not even when her dad had taken her to an aviary as a kid. She hadn't liked it, being shut in with the birds, the squawks, the caws, the flapping of tiny wings. That was nothing compared to the sound from outside. Now that she was aware of it, she could hear nothing else.

Charlotte unfurled her legs, pushing herself up from the floor. She went to pull back the curtain, but stopped. What was she afraid of? What did she think she would see?

This was ridiculous. There was nothing to be scared of. Just a bunch of kids in stupid masks playing a stupid trick. Before she could change her mind, Charlotte slid back the door.

She jumped out of the van, her trainers sinking into soft earth instead of hard paving stones. She fell back, whacking her head on Velma's door. She landed on her back, and swore for the second time in ten minutes, rubbing the back of her aching head. The air was warm and close, her clothes sticking to her skin.

Charlotte opened her eyes, looked around and started screaming all over again.

Chapter 16

Half a Lifetime

'Make us a brew, will you? I'm gasping.'

Rob stood, rubbing his aching back. The frame for the patio doors was in, but had been a pig of a job. Lady Muck better not change her mind again, not after all that.

Still stretching, he walked through to the kitchen, where Tim was boiling a kettle using the portable generator, Little Mix's latest hit blasting out of the radio.

'Turn that rubbish off, will you?'

Tim grinned, showing a row of gapped teeth. 'You love 'em.'

Rob wasn't in the mood for banter. 'Just do it, eh? My head's banging.'

'Fair enough,' Tim said, killing the radio.

That was better. Much better.

'How's it going upstairs?' Rob asked.

The kettle clicked off and Tim poured steaming water into two mugs, teabags floating to the surface. 'Darrel's nearly finished the floorboards in the front bedroom. Still complaining that he's cold, though.'

'Poor little lamb. We'll have to get him a hot water bottle.'

Tim sniggered, passing over one of the mugs, a red devil emblazoned on its side. 'Here you go.'

'You're having a laugh, aren't you,' said Rob, refusing to take the tea. 'Unless you want me to smash it.'

'You should come down Old Trafford next week,' Tim said, offering the other mug. 'See some proper football for once.'

Rob took the mug and blew across the murky brown liquid. 'Keep dreaming. Besides, if Marter has his way we'll be working every hour between now and December first.' He took a sip of the tea. 'Still can't work out where he went.'

'He's not here, though,' Tim said, drinking from the red devil mug. 'That's the important thing.'

Rob snorted. 'You're not as thick as you look.'

There was a cry from behind them, and a dull thud.

'Darrel?' Rob called out, turning around. 'That you?'

'What's that, mate?' Darrel shouted down from upstairs, his thick Liverpudlian accent unmistakable.

Rob exchanged a look with Tim and then walked out into the hall. Where had that come from? He headed back into the living room and nearly dropped his tea.

'What is it?' Tim said, following him into the room.

'Hold this,' Rob said, thrusting his mug into Tim's hands.

Scolding water slopped over Tim's fingers. 'Ow! Watch it!'

But Rob didn't apologise. Instead he ran to the body that was slumped beside the patio doors, a body that hadn't been there five minutes before.

It was wearing the same coat that Harold Marter had worn earlier that morning, but this one was tattered and torn, hanging loose on a thin frame. It was a man, he could tell that, although the silver hair was long and matted. Rob bent down and gently rolled him onto his back.

'Are you all right, mate? Can you hear …'

The words died in his throat.

'Is that Marter?' Tim asked, dripping tea all over the floor as he stared at the man's face. 'What's happened to him?'

'Beats me,' Rob admitted, snatching his mobile phone from his tool box and calling 999.

The call connected almost immediately, a woman's voice asking what service he required.

'Ambulance, I guess,' he replied. 'It's hard to know.'

Not far away, Bill was struggling to keep up with the Doctor. He was marching along the high street with a face like several thunder storms rolled into one.

'I'll teach her to put me online,' he snarled.

'I think she already knows,' Bill said, trying to lighten the mood.

It didn't work. In fact, the mood seemed to become several tons heavier.

'There's a reason the unexplained remains unexplained. People don't need to see it. They don't need to know what horrors are crawling around beneath their noses. Not when there are people like me to deal with them. In secret. Away from the spotlight. Before we know it, this place is going to be crawling with stickybeaks and fruitcakes …'

'That's a technical term, is it?'

'Yes,' the Doctor insisted. 'For people who think they want to see monsters until the monster swallows them. And that's when the real trouble starts. Before you know it, they're needing to be rescued, wanting selfies ...'

'Selfies? With you?'

He shot her a look that measured 9.9 on the Richter scale. 'Why not me? People know me. The wrong sort of people.'

'I can believe it.'

'People who spend too much time on forums arguing about conspiracy theories and dating controversies.'

'Fruitcakes.'

'You've got it.'

They turned onto Brownie Hill, the turning to Bugs Close just ahead. An ambulance was parked outside the building site.

'What's happening over there?' Bill asked.

'Not our concern,' the Doctor replied, as a police car screamed past and screeched to a halt beside the ambulance. The door opened and the driver got out, slipping a hat over her neat blonde hair.

'It's PC Schofield,' Bill said, but the Doctor had already changed direction, charging towards the emergency vehicles. Bill waited for a car to pass before following him. 'What happened to it not being our concern?'

'The constable might need our help,' the Doctor called back over his shoulder, slowing to a walking pace so as not to look eager.

'Yeah, good plan,' Bill said, as they reached the muddy patch that would one day be a front drive. 'Don't want to look like a stickybeak.' She leant in closer and whispered: 'It's too late for the fruitcake bit.'

Their path was blocked by an acne-ridden builder in a Man U hoodie and a hard hat. 'Sorry, mate. You can't come in here.'

'Ah yes. Health and Safety,' said the Doctor, plucking the helmet from the guy's head and shoving it on his own. 'Very wise.' He hopped onto a network of wooden planks that had been laid to provide a walkway to the house beyond. 'Come on, Bill. We'll find you one inside.'

They hurried on before the builder could stop them, the Doctor holding aside the plastic sheeting so Bill could enter. Once through, he noticed a pile of discarded helmets and, with the skill of a Covent Garden juggler, kicked one up into his hand. Passing it to Bill, he followed PC Schofield's voice.

'What are *you* doing here?' she asked as they found her in a crowded back room, talking to another builder, older than the kid out front, maybe early-to-mid forties and wearing a T-shirt, fleece gilet and jeans.

'Helping with inquiries,' the Doctor replied, looking not at the police officer but at the paramedics who were lifting an elderly man onto a wheeled stretcher. 'And you're welcome.'

'Sorry? Who are these guys?' asked the builder. 'Are they with you?'

'Yes,' said the Doctor at the exact moment that Schofield said, 'No.'

The Doctor looked hurt. 'Constable, after all we've been through.'

Schofield called through the patio doors into the garden. 'PC Turman?'

The large male police officer from the night before appeared at the opening.

'Oh, hello again,' said the Doctor.

'Everything all right?' Turman asked.

Schofield gave him a curt smile. 'Can you escort the Doctor and Miss Potts outside, and make sure to remind them about the perils of interfering in police business?'

If the Doctor heard the threat, he didn't respond to it. Instead he pointed at the man on the stretcher. 'What happened to him?'

'Good question,' the builder muttered.

'You know him?' the Doctor asked.

'You don't have to answer his questions, Mr Hawker,' Schofield pointed out.

'Quite right,' the Doctor agreed. 'Although it might just save everyone's time if you do. Who is he? A rough sleeper?'

'Not exactly,' Rob replied. 'He owns this place, or he will when it's finished.'

'He owns all this?' The Doctor did a double take. 'Have you seen the state of his jeans? I've seen Swiss cheese with fewer holes. What is he? An eccentric millionaire?'

'Sir, please,' Turman insisted. 'You need to step outside.'

'Yes, yes, I will,' the Doctor said. 'In a minute. I'm just finding this all terribly interesting.' He turned suddenly to Bill. 'She is too, aren't you, Bill?'

Shocked to be brought so abruptly into the conversation, but recognising the Doctor's delaying tactic, Bill agreed.

'Yeah. Totally. Can't get enough.'

The builder scratched the back of his head. 'One minute he was there, the next he was gone. Flash of light. Vanished.'

'When was this?' the Doctor asked.

'A couple of hours ago. Maybe three. He was here to check on the work—'

'And then he disappeared, only to reappear when? Mr Hawker, it's vitally important that you tell me exactly when he came back.'

'Rob,' the builder said, throwing them all for a moment. 'The name's Rob. Mr Hawker sounds like my dad.'

'Rob it is,' the Doctor said. 'And to repeat my question …'

Rob shrugged. 'Half an hour ago?'

The Doctor turned his attention to the paramedics. 'What shape is he in?'

'He's had a heart attack,' the smaller of the two replied, a woman with fiery red hair. 'We need to get him out to the ambulance.' She nodded to her colleague, an Asian guy with a neat beard and glasses. 'Raise on three. One … two … *three*.'

They lifted the stretcher with practised skill, telescopic legs folding down so he could be wheeled out of the building.

The Doctor sniffed as if smelling wine.

'You got a cold?' Schofield asked.

'What's his name?' came his question in reply.

'Harold Marter.'

The Doctor held out his hand to Bill. 'Can I borrow your phone?'

She slipped it out of her pocket. 'Sure. Why?'

'I want to send embarrassing messages from your Facebook account,' he said, grabbing it and typing in her PIN.

'Hey, how do you know my PIN?'

'Your mum's date of birth.'

'That's *supposed* to be private.'

'Yeah, sorry. You probably need to change it.'

Bill peeked over his arm as he tapped Marter's name into a search engine. He checked through the results and selected the third from the top, thrusting the phone back into Bill's hand.

'Clear the way, please,' the red-haired paramedic asked, and the Doctor stood back. As the stretcher trundled past, Bill looking up from her screen to see Harold Marter's face.

'That's not right.'

'What isn't?' Schofield asked her.

'He's old,' Bill said. 'Really old. Even older than the Doctor.'

'Steady,' the Doctor warned.

'But I mean, look …' She held up the webpage the Doctor had found. It showed local businessman Harold Marter accepting an award at a formal dinner. He was in his forties, his skin pale against the dinner jacket, but classically handsome, with dark hair stylishly slicked back.

The Harold Marter on the stretcher had the craggy, walnut-coloured hide of a man who'd spent a lifetime outdoors. His hair was long and grey, his once rugged chin covered by a long tousled beard.

'Yeah, that's what he looked like this morning,' Rob said, pointing at the photo on the screen.

'This morning?' the Doctor exclaimed, rushing out of the room. 'I knew it.'

'Knew what?' Schofield called after him. 'Doctor, come back!'

He stopped at the front door and threw his hard hat back onto the pile. 'Get out, come back. You need to make up your mind.'

Outside, the wheels of the stretcher caught on one of the planks.

'Here, let me,' the Doctor said, making a grab for the stretcher. 'Many hands make light work.'

'We're fine, sir,' the female paramedic told him. 'Thank you.'

'I'm sure you are,' the Doctor said, peering in close at Marter's haggard face. 'But he's not.'

Bill pushed through the plastic sheeting to join them. 'What happened to him?'

'Old age,' the Doctor replied.

'What? Fifty years in two hours?'

The Doctor shrugged. 'Not everyone ages as well as me.'

'Sir, please,' the paramedic said. 'If you could step out of the way.'

'Sorry, yes of course,' the Doctor said, stepping off the plank into the mud.

The paramedics pushed the stretcher on, the wheels bouncing as they passed from one length of wood to another. Marter groaned through his oxygen mask.

'He's awake!' Bill said.

The Doctor leapt back onto the walkway, grabbing the edge of the stretcher. He leant in close to the old man and whispered hurriedly into his ear. 'What did you see, Harold? Where did you go?'

The man's bloodshot eyes rolled in their sockets. 'The colours,' he rasped. 'What's happened to the colours?'

The female paramedic looked for the police officers. 'A little help here?'

'No need,' the Doctor said, stepping away again. 'On you go. Get him to hospital, much good it will do him.'

'What does that mean?' Bill asked.

'A good question,' Schofield agreed, coming out of the house. 'Doctor?'

The Doctor fixed the police officer with a doom-laden stare. 'Time's catching up with him. I can smell it.'

'Smell what?'

'A wasted life. Harold Master has lived out his three score years and ten in one morning. No wonder his heart's broken.'

Chapter 17

A Groove in Time

The Doctor rushed back into the house, finding Rob standing in the hallway. 'There you are. Tell me, where was Harold when he vanished?'

The builder shook his head. 'I don't know. I grabbed a hard hat for him, went into the living room and—'

'And found it empty. Show me.'

'Just hang on a minute,' PC Schofield said, pushing through the plastic. 'This isn't your investigation.'

The Doctor stepped up to the police woman. 'Constable, did you ever meet Mr Marter before today?'

Schofield sighed, already used to the Doctor's whims. 'Yes. There was a break-in at his warehouse a month or two ago.'

The Doctor pulled the plastic sheeting aside so they could see the stretcher in the back of the ambulance. 'And did he look like that old man out there?'

'No,' she admitted. 'But that's not Harold Marter. It can't be.'

'It looks like him,' Bill said. 'Well, sort of.'

Schofield was approaching the end of her tether at speed. 'That man must be 90 if he's a day.'

'Older,' the Doctor agreed. 'But he wasn't when he woke up this morning.'

'People don't age in the blink of an eye.'

'He did,' the Doctor said, producing a black wallet, its leather cracked and brittle.

'What's that?' Schofield asked.

'Evidence,' the Doctor told her. 'I took it from Marter before they put him in the ambulance.'

'You pickpocketed a man on a stretcher?' Bill asked. 'Classy.'

'How could you do that?' Schofield said, her face creased in disbelief.

'He was strapped down,' the Doctor explained, 'It's trickier when they're moving about.'

Bill wanted to kick him. This really wasn't the time to be provocative, but he just couldn't help himself.

Schofield snatched the wallet from his hand. 'I could have you arrested.'

'But you won't. Not when you look in there.'

The police officer opened the wallet and examined the contents. 'Cash … Credit cards …'

'In what name?' the Doctor asked.

Schofield sighed as she answered. 'H. Marter.'

'Any photos?'

'You already know there are.'

'Show me.'

She held up the wallet, showing a photo behind a plastic window. It was a holiday snap, a family of four on a glistening white beach. Happier times. There was no mistaking the man. It was Harold Marter. The *young* Harold Marter.

'That's the man you met a few weeks ago, isn't it, Constable?'

'Yes,' Schofield confirmed through gritted teeth.

'Who is *exactly* the same man that was just wheeled out of here.' He shook his head. 'Nobody blames you.'

'For what?' she said, chin jutting out.

The look he gave her was kind, but firm. 'You're out of your depth, but I'm not. I swim these waters every day. I know what I'm talking about.'

Schofield turned to Bill. 'Is that true? Does he?'

Bill looked at the Doctor and then back to the police officer. 'It's hard to believe sometimes, but yeah, he does.'

Schofield held up a hand, either in surrender or as a marker of time, Bill couldn't tell. 'Five minutes,' she said, standing out of the Doctor's way. 'That's all you have. Any longer, and I'll remember how you got hold of this wallet.'

'Thank you,' he said, before asking Rob to take them to the back room.

'And you didn't actually see him disappear,' the Doctor asked as soon as they were inside.

'No, we were in the hallway.'

'But how did you feel?'

Rob frowned. 'You what?'

'How did you feel? Nervous? Scared? Like you couldn't move?'

The builder shook his head. 'No, nothing like that. Just confused. We didn't know where he'd gone.'

The Doctor stepped over to the patio windows. 'And this is where he reappeared?' he said, pointing down at the concrete floor. 'Right here.'

'That's right. He was lying on his face.'

'And again, you weren't scared at all. No trepidation or dread. No sudden attack of the collywobbles?'

Rob looked at Bill for support. 'Does he always talk like this?'

She nodded. ''Fraid so.'

Rob looked down at the floor, reliving the moment. 'We were surprised. I mean, you've seen him …'

'But not scared?'

'No.'

The Doctor dropped to a crouch, running his hand across the concrete. 'Two more questions. When did you lay this floor?'

'Beginning of last week.'

The Doctor pulled the sonic screwdriver out of his pocket and used its light to illuminate a large circle, about a metre wide. It was scored into the floor, like someone had taken a knife to the concrete. 'And what about this? Noticed it before today?'

Rob dropped down beside the Doctor, feeling the groove in the concrete himself. 'That definitely wasn't there. I skimmed this floor myself.'

The Doctor pointed across the room with the sonic. 'There's another over there, probably where Marter vanished.'

'What are they?' Bill asked, bending over to take a closer look.

The Doctor stood up, tapping the sonic against his lips as he explained. 'They're usually found in woods; circles in the grass, marked out by either a ring of mushrooms or scorched earth where nothing can grow. In France, they call them sorcerer rings, in Germany, a witch's circle. Here, they're known as elf or goblin rings.'

'Goblins?' Bill asked. 'Like Boggarts?'

'What's a Boggart?' Schofield asked from the door.

The Doctor held up a finger towards the police officer without looking at her. 'One thing at a time, Constable. I'm on a tight schedule, remember.' He turned back to Bill. 'Back in the time of the Fairy Finder, the locals of Huckensall village would have believed that the rings were caused by the passage of elven feet, the Fair Folk cavorting with witches and warlocks.'

'And was it?'

'What?' Schofield half-laughed behind them.

'Not exactly,' the Doctor said, ignoring her. 'Elf rings are like scorch marks on a launch site. They're what's left behind when a portal opens in the veil.'

'Between the Invisible and the Visible,' Bill realised.

Beside them, Rob Hawker turned to Schofield. 'I'm sorry, but is this guy soft in the head? What's he talking about?'

The Doctor grabbed Bill's arm and glanced at her watch. 'Sorry, would love to explain, but my time's up.'

'Your time?' Schofield asked.

He guided Bill out of the doorway, ignoring the stunned looks of the others. 'Five minutes. That's what you gave me and, would you believe it, I've rattled on for six minutes and twenty-three seconds. Shocking.' He called over his shoulder. 'Don't worry, I'll throw myself out.'

Schofield went to call him back, but was interrupted by the builders, who wanted to know what they should do – carry on working, or down tools? The Doctor made good of the distraction and a few minutes later he and Bill were across the planks and walking down Brownie Hill.

'Doctor, slow down,' Bill said, chasing after him.

'I can't,' he replied. 'This is bad. Worse than I thought.'

She grabbed his arm, stopping him. 'Worse how?'

'You heard him back there, didn't you? Rob the Builder.'

'Yes, but—'

'But you didn't listen. He wasn't scared. When Harold Marter was dragged through an elf ring, Rob's colly wasn't even wobbled. Now, remember how you felt when we came face to face with the Shining Men in the woods. You were frightened out of your wits.'

'You know I was.'

'Exactly: overwhelming anxiety, the sensation of being paralysed. Plus, there's the elf rings in the wood.'

'What about them?'

'There weren't any. All those Shining Men popping up between the trees and not a mark on the ground. No elf rings. No portals. Conclusion?'

Bill's eyes widened as realisation dawned. 'The Shining Men aren't Boggarts.'

'Got it in one.' He gave her that special smile he reserved for moments when she got things right, although this time the pride was tinged with self-recrimination. 'I thought

I had it all worked out, that Shining Men were Boggarts breaking into this realm. But what if I was wrong?'

'I thought you were never wrong?' Bill joked, wanting to make him feel better.

It didn't work. 'Everyone's wrong from time to time,' he snapped. 'Being wrong is the first step to getting things right. As long as it's not already too late.'

'That doesn't sound good.'

'It wasn't supposed to. Different forces are at play, and if we're not careful, this entire neighbourhood will be caught in the crossfire. Maybe even the entire world.'

'So if the Shining Men didn't take Marter, who did? And why'd he look so old?'

'Time's a funny thing,' the Doctor said, wringing his hand together. 'Depending on where you are, it doesn't always follow the same rules. Ultra-terrestrials like fairies and Boggarts exist on a different plain of existence.'

'Like a different dimension.'

'More like a different groove, running alongside our own.'

'And time works differently there?'

'A minute in our universe can be a year in theirs. Sometimes even longer. If Marter was taken into the Invisible …'

'He lived out the rest of his life in the fairy realm. Fifty years …'

'Whereas only an hour or so had passed here.'

'Is that what's happened to Mum?' said a voice from behind them.

They turned to see Masie and Noah, looking up at them, tears in their eyes. 'Has she been taken away by fairies?'

Chapter 18

Clues

The Doctor dropped into a crouch, putting his hands on the children's shoulders. 'How long have you been listening?'

'Long enough,' Masie said, stepping back to break away. 'So is that what's happened?'

'Has your mum jumped a groove in time?'

She nodded, her eyes fixed on him.

'I don't think so.' The Doctor glanced over her shoulder, seeing both police officers and builders emerge from Marter's house. 'Come on,' he said, standing and holding out his hands. The children took them and he led them across the road and back into Bugs Close.

'Where are we going?' Bill asked.

'Away from Constables Schofield and Turman. I have enough questions of my own without facing more from them. That should be far enough.'

He sat himself on a garden wall two doors down from the children's house and patted the brickwork, urging them to join him. Noah complied, but Masie remained standing, her hands crammed in her jean pockets.

Bill glanced along the close, looking for Velma, but Charlotte's camper van was nowhere to be seen. She probably didn't want the Doctor to know where she was, which was wise, although at the moment he was giving his full attention to Sammy Holland's son.

'Noah,' he said, softly. 'Your dream that wasn't a dream ...'

'What about it?' Masie answered sharply for her brother.

The Doctor continued, his impossibly old eyes looking at the boy with genuine compassion. 'She wasn't really there, your mum.'

'I thought you believed me,' Noah whined, eyes brimming.

'I do,' the Doctor told him quickly. 'You saw her, but that wasn't her body, only her mind.'

'What do you mean?'

'Your mum reached out to you from wherever she is.'

'Like astral projection,' Bill offered.

The Doctor glanced up at her, both shocked and impressed. 'Well, yes. Exactly that.'

She shrugged, giving him an embarrassed smile. '*Doctor Strange*. You should watch it. It's good.'

'It is,' Masie agreed begrudgingly.

The Doctor raised his eyebrows. 'In which case, I'll give it ago. Praise from Masie Holland is a rare thing indeed.'

The girl dropped her hair in front of her face, trying not to smile.

'Now,' the Doctor continued. 'Tell me more about this footprint in Noah's room. You both saw it.'

Masie nodded. 'And the leaf.'

'What kind of leaf was it?'

'I think it was oak,' Noah said, scratching his eye.

The Doctor was nodding, taking it all in. 'The tricky thing to understand is that neither the footprint or the leaf was there either. Not really. They were … echoes of her cry for help, that faded over time.'

'Which is why they were gone when you brought us home,' Masie said.

'I could still taste it, though, when I licked the carpet.'

Noah screwed up his nose. 'That was disgusting.'

'You're telling me,' said the Doctor, prodding Noah in the stomach and making him laugh. 'Someone needs to wash their feet more often.'

Bill was still trying to get her head around all this. 'So their mum was, what, calling out to them from the Invisible?'

'You mentioned that before,' cut in Masie. 'What is it?'

'The Invisible?' The doctor replied. 'A world just beyond our own.'

'Fairyland,' Noah offered.

'More or less. But I don't think that's what happened. I'm not sure a human could call across the veil between worlds.'

'You don't know?' Masie asked.

'I can't be expected to know everything. No one knows everything.'

'Nan does,' Noah said.

The Doctor considered this. 'Yeah, I can believe that. Either way, wherever she is, your mum is linked to the Shining Man.'

'He took her,' Noah said. 'Dragging her into a hole.'

'Leaving behind an oak leaf.' The Doctor pulled a small notebook from his jacket. 'Could you draw it for me?'

'The leaf?' Noah asked.

'Yeah. I have a pencil here somewhere ...' The Doctor patted down his pockets before reaching forward and pulling a stubby yellow pencil from Noah's ear. 'Ah. There it is!'

Noah chuckled and took the notebook and pencil. The Doctor winked at Bill as the boy knelt on the floor so he could lean the pad against the low wall.

Noah began to draw, first sketching a long stem and then adding pairs of narrow, oval-shaped leaves on either side. 'There,' he said, passing the notebook back to the Doctor.

'And that's the leaf you saw too,' the Doctor said, showing the drawing to Masie.

She nodded. 'Yeah, pretty much. But it wasn't green.'

'Yeah. It looked dead,' Noah said. 'All curled up and brown.'

'What do you think?' the Doctor asked, turning the notepad towards Bill.

She didn't really know what to say. 'It's a good drawing.'

'It is,' the Doctor agreed, studying the picture. 'A very good drawing. You've got talent, Noah, although I'd brush up on your botany, if I were you.'

'Why?' Noah asked, frowning.

The Doctor held up the notepad again. 'Because that's not an oak leaf. That's either from an ash or more probably—'

'A rowan!' Bill cut in, excitedly. 'It's a leaf from a rowan tree, isn't it?'

'What difference does it make?' Masie asked.

'The Doctor told me all about rowan trees,' Bill told her. 'The wood from the rowan tree interferes with fairy magic—'

'Fairy science,' the Doctor corrected her.

'Whatever. It's a natural defence. Something to put the world right.'

'But what's this got to do with Mum?' Noah asked.

'It's a clue,' the Doctor said. 'You've read Sherlock Holmes, haven't you?'

'The guy on the telly?'

'The world's greatest detective!'

Noah looked confused. 'I thought that was Batman?'

The Doctor looked as though he was about to argue but thought better of it. For once. 'It doesn't matter. Sherlock Holmes and Batman follow clues.'

'And punch people,' Masie pointed out.

'Let's stick to the clues bit for now,' the Doctor said. 'You two go with Bill.'

'Why?' Bill asked. 'Where are we going?'

'Back into the woods,' the Doctor told her.

'Where we saw the Shining Men?' she asked. 'You sure that's a good idea?'

He rolled his eyes and pointed to the sky. 'See that big ball of fire in the sky? It's daytime. Shining Men only come out at night.'

'And you're sure about that, are you?'

'No, but you can tell me if you see one.' He thrust the notebook into her hands. 'Go back to the woods and look for rowan trees.'

'What about you?'

The Doctor looked back towards the end of the road. 'Sammy Holland always liked fairy stories,' he said. 'I think it's time I found out why.'

Chapter 19

Taking a Dip

'Looking forward to writing this one up?' Turman said, flashing Schofield a grin.

'Thought I'd leave that to you,' she joked, although it wasn't funny. What the hell *were* they going to say?

Well, Sarge, it's like this. The guy got old. Really, really quickly.

She didn't want to believe it. How could she? But the Doctor was right. The old man on the stretcher *was* Harold Marter. She didn't know how, and she sure as hell didn't know why, but something terrible had happened to the poor sod.

She hadn't liked Marter when she'd met him. He'd been too cocksure, too quick to tell her how to do her job, but still ...

She couldn't stop thinking about how his breath had rattled in his throat when he'd been taken out by the paramedics, how his rheumy eyes had searched the sky as if he didn't recognise it any more.

'We better get down to the hospital,' she told Turman as Rob Hawker walked out of the house, a mobile phone to his ear.

'Yeah, thanks. Will do.'

The builder cut off the call.

'That was Harold Marter's brother,' he told her. 'He says to pack up for the day.'

'Makes sense,' Schofield said. 'We'll get out of your hair, although we may have more questions.'

'You and me both. Where does this all leave us?'

'Knocking off early,' Turman joked. Schofield fought the urge to smack him around the back of the head. Turman could be such a jerk at times.

'Hey! What do you think you're doing?'

The shout came from the back of the building site.

'Now what?' Rob Hawker groaned, and ran back into the house.

'We better see what's wrong,' Schofield told Turman, and they followed Hawker through to the back garden where an argument was still raging.

'You shouldn't be here,' yelled the spotty kid in the United hoodie.

'Then pretend I'm not,' said another voice. An annoyingly familiar *Scottish* voice. 'Haven't you got a shovel to lean on?'

The garden was huge, bigger than Schofield's entire flat. The ground was a mud bath, churned up by yesterday's rain, crates of building materials and tools scattered around. A long brick outhouse ran along the bottom of the plot, in front of a wire fence that she imagined would soon be replaced by bushes or trees, if work ever continued after the events of this morning. Like the main build itself, the walls of the outhouse had been built, and double doors fitted, but windows had yet to be installed, plastic sheets stretched over the gaps.

The Doctor was on his knees in front of the building, scooping up handfuls of mud like a dog digging for a bone.

'What's he doing here?' Hawker asked.

'Minding my own business,' the Doctor replied, not looking up from his work. 'I suggest you give it a go.'

'This *is* my business,' Hawker said, stalking towards the man. The frustration and confusion of the morning were quickly boiling away to anger. If the Doctor wasn't careful, he'd end up buried in the mud. 'You need to leave.'

'And I will,' the Doctor told him. 'Just not yet.'

'Lost something?' Schofield asked, hooking her thumbs beneath her vest as she watched the strange display.

'Yes,' he said, glancing up at them, his hands caked with dirt. 'A tree. You haven't seen one, have you?'

'What?' Rob Hawker demanded.

The Doctor rose to his feet, wiping his hands on a tartan handkerchief. 'A tree. Big thing, lots of branches.'

Hawker's hands tightened into fists. 'I know what a tree is!'

'Excellent. There used to be one here, in this garden. Sammy Holland climbed it when she was a little girl.'

'The missing woman?' Turman asked.

The Doctor shoved the muddy handkerchief into his pocket. 'Missing woman. Missing tree. You're a careless bunch, aren't you?'

'There was a tree,' the spotty lad confirmed. Schofield thought his name was Tim. 'But it was cut down.'

The Doctor looked appalled. 'You cut it down?'

'No. A bloke came to do it.'

'A bloke. Very helpful.'

'A tree surgeon.'

'And what happened to the tree, after it was butchered?'

'They took it away,' Rob Hawker told him. 'But what's it to you?'

'What indeed?' the Doctor said, walking towards him, seemingly oblivious to the irritation that was coming off the foreman in waves. 'Can you remember what kind of tree it was?'

'What does it matter?' Hawker shrugged.

The Doctor looked to the sky in desperation. 'What does it matter? What does it *matter*? It matters because that tree might just be the most important tree in the world!' The last three words were punctuated by a finger jabbed against the builder's barrel chest.

Hawker slapped the Doctor's hand away, looking as though he wanted to do the same to the Scotsman's hawkish face. 'Touch me again and you'll have more to worry about than a tree.'

'OK, that's enough,' Schofield said, stepping between them. 'Both of you.'

'I'm sorry,' the Doctor said, surprising her. She wouldn't have thought such a word was in his vocabulary. He turned back to Hawker. 'Just humour me, please.'

'Why should I?' Hawker said.

'Because I'm an idiot. You think it, PC Schofield thinks it, even I think it most of the time. Humour an idiot with his idiotic questions.'

Schofield didn't buy the Doctor's self-deprecation for a minute, but it had the desired effect. Hawker was mollified, looking at her for guidance.

'Just answer him,' she said, wanting to know where the Doctor was going with all this.

Hawker shrugged. 'I don't know.'

The Doctor kept pushing, searching Hawker's face eagerly. 'Was it a rowan?' He counted off characteristics on his fingers. 'Silver bark. Leaves like feathers. Scarlet berries with a star.'

'I told you. I can't remember.'

'OK, let's try something else. Where was it? You can remember that, surely?' He indicated the ground beneath their feet. 'Here?'

'No.' Hawker pointed towards the large outbuilding. 'It was over there, but it's not any more.'

The Doctor looked aghast. 'You built over it? No! Tell me you didn't build over it!'

'Of course we did,' Tim piped up, picking his nose as he spoke. He was a right charmer, that one. 'What were we supposed to do? Build the swimming pool *around* it?'

Now it was the Doctor's turn to point at the structure. 'That's a swimming pool?' He rushed towards the building.

'Oh no you don't,' Hawker shouted after him. 'You can't go in there.'

But the Doctor was already inside.

'Doctor, why's the tree so important?' Schofield asked, stopping the door from springing back into their faces as they followed him in.

The pool was already installed, sunk deep into the ground, although it had yet to be filled. They were standing at the midway point, the deep end to the left, the shallow end to the right. The slope connecting the two ends was steep. At its lowest point, the pit had to be around three metres in depth.

'I told you,' the Doctor replied to her. 'I'm an idiot. It's easy to miss things. Life moves so fast. But something Sammy's mum said. Something about the tree.'

As if that explained everything, the Doctor turned and jumped from the edge of the pool, landing halfway down the slope.

'That does it,' Hawker growled. 'I'm sorry, but I need him out of here.' Before Schofield could stop him, the builder had also leapt into the empty pool.

The Doctor was striding towards the deep end, sweeping a green torch across the tiled floor. 'It's hard to get rid of a tree,' he told them. 'Trees are stubborn. They always leave something behind. Roots, seeds and secrets, buried beneath the ground.'

Hawker caught up with him, grabbing him by the arm. 'What is that thing?'

'Mine,' the Doctor retorted like a small child, snatching his arm away.

Schofield and Turner were already running to the shallow end, both wanting to break up the fight before it happened, but neither wanting to risk breaking an ankle by leaping into the deep end. Jumping into a pool filled with water was one thing, landing awkwardly on hard tiles was another.

There were steps leading down into the shallow end. Turman took them two at a time, racing down the slope towards the two men who were already locked in a struggle. Schofield didn't fancy the Doctor's chances.

Hawker looked like he could handle himself in a scrap, while the Scotsman was as thin as a rake beneath his long coat.

Turman got there first, hauling the Doctor back, while Schofield tackled Hawker, putting a restraining hand on his forearm.

She didn't know what hit her. Hawker hardly flinched and yet she was knocked off her feet, flying halfway towards the shallow end. She landed painfully, jolting her hip, her hat rolling away.

What the hell had just happened? Had Hawker hit her, or shoved her aside in the heat of the moment? Either way, how strong *was* the guy?

There was shouting from the deep end. Turman had pushed Hawker back, yelling at him to calm down.

'That wasn't me,' the builder insisted. 'I didn't even touch her.'

'He's not lying,' the Doctor agreed, waving that damned torch of his in the air. 'He didn't do that. Not unless he's secretly a superhero or a Zygon.' He passed the glowing torch in front of the outraged builder. 'Nope. He's as human as you are.'

'Well, something just happened!' Turman contended, keeping himself between the two men. He glanced towards Schofield, who was trying not to wince as she got back to her feet. 'You all right?'

She rubbed her throbbing leg, imagining the peach of a bruise she'd have in the morning. 'Nothing broken.'

'Nothing broken *yet*,' the Doctor corrected her, before he too was thrown back like a rag doll tossed across the room by a tantruming child. But no one had been near him. Not Hawker. Not Turman. He crashed into the wall with enough force to crack the tiles, narrowly missing the metal ladder that led down to the deep end to slide down to the floor.

Schofield tried to limp towards him, but couldn't. It wasn't her leg that was slowing her down. She was fighting against a gust of wind that had blown up from nowhere.

When she was a kid, her grandparents had taken her to Blackpool for a weekend to give her mum and dad a break. It had been off-season, the beach a no-go, thanks to the weather which had bordered on apocalyptic. Her grandad had larked about on the prom, making her squeal with laughter as he battled to walk against the wind, her grandmother nagging him to be careful. At one point, he'd leant forward, the wind holding him at a 45-degree angle. He'd always been a clown.

But there was nothing funny about this. It was like trying to shove herself through a brick wall. But they were inside. Where had the wind come from, and how could it be so strong?

She screwed her eyes tight against the grit that had been whipped up by the sudden storm. She heard Turman and Hawker cry out but couldn't see what had happened to them. She was pushed back and fell, rolling like tumbleweed to slam against the style. She scrabbled against the smooth porcelain tiles, trying desperately to find a grip, anything to hold on to. Her nails dug into the grout between the tiles, but it was no good. She was being dragged back towards the deep end, the wind forming a vortex inside the empty pool. There was a ripping sound from above. The plastic sheets had been torn from the windows, sucked into the whirling mass of air. They joined dirt, paper and fragments of broken tiles whipping around. She had builders' sand in her mouth, grit in her eyes and nothing to hold on to. Her palms squeaked against the tiles as she was pulled back, the wind roaring in her ears. She cried out in fear, but couldn't hear herself. Instead, there were voices in the wind; howls both angry and sorrowful at the same time.

'Where is the Lost? Where is the Lost?'

She tumbled backwards, her head cracking against the wall. There was no way to stop, no way to anchor herself down. She smashed against the tiles, winding herself. What had the Doctor said? *Nothing broken yet.* Is that what would happen? Would the storm snap every bone in her body? She had no idea what was happening to the others; no idea which way was up or down. All she knew was that she was spinning, around and around, as if caught in a fairground ride from hell. Scream if you want to go faster. Scream if you're going to die.

Scream if you want the voices to stop.

'Where is the Lost? Where is the Lost?'

Fingers locked around her arm. She jolted to a halt, her eyes flicking open.

It was the Doctor! He'd caught hold of her wrist, his other arm hooked around the metal ladder, holding them both against the wind.

Pain was etched across his lined face, but he wouldn't let go. She forced her other arm forward, grabbing hold of his wrist. He was yelling something, his words drowned out by the same question repeated over and over again on the wind:

'Where is the Lost? Where is the Lost?'

They jolted forwards. The ladder was coming away from the side of the pool. The metal bent out of shape, the Doctor's arm still looped around the twisted frame, and then it ripped loose. They flew into the wind, hanging on to each other, spinning around like a sycamore seed caught in a tornado.

She wanted to close her eyes, but the Doctor had them fixed with his. His mouth was moving, but she couldn't hear the words. He reached into his jacket with his free hand, pulling out that strange torch of his, only to cry out in despair as it was snatched from his fingers.

They struck something hard. Pain shot through Schofield's already bruised hip. She held on to the Doctor's arm, even though she could barely see his face. The air was full of dust and debris, the roar of the storm a solid wall of noise. They pitched down and Schofield imagined their bodies being dashed across the bottom of the pool.

Please don't let go, she thought, not knowing if she was talking to the Doctor or herself. *Please don't let g—*

There was a crunch. There was pain. The Doctor's hand slipped from her grasp and everything stopped.

Chapter 20

Turman's Report

Later, PC Turman would make his report. He would say how he had been pressed against the side of the pool, crushed by the wind. He would find out what had happened to Rob Hawker only when he was admitted to the hospital himself: how the builder had been thrown free from the building, breaking his legs on one of the window frames.

Turman had seen the Doctor try to save Schofield, grabbing her hand. Even then, in the middle of such madness, he'd been impressed by the older man's reactions, how he must have calculated exactly when to throw out his arm, grabbing Schofield as she sped past.

Not that it had done them any good.

The ladder ripped away from the tiles and they span into the air. Turman had called Schofield's name, even as they ploughed into the bottom of the pool.

There'd been a flash of light. Blinding. Hot against his skin.

And then all was calm. The wind. The dirt. Even the voices that he knew he must have imagined. They were all gone.

A sheet of transparent plastic slapped against him, covering him like a shroud. He pushed it aside, forced himself to crawl back up the slope toward the shallow end. He was bleeding, his uniform shredded from the shards of broken tiles that had sliced past him in the storm. All he wanted to do was rest, to sleep, but he needed to see what had happened to Schofield. Needed to see her body.

Because he already knew she was dead. The Doctor too. They had to be. The force of the impact. The sound of them hitting the floor. Nothing could survive that.

They weren't there.

Schofield. The Doctor. They were gone. All that was left was Schofield's hat and the Doctor's torch, smashed into little pieces against the floor.

That's what he'd thought, until he stood up.

That's when he spotted it, etched deep into the tiles.

It was a circle.

A large circle spreading out from the exact point they had fallen.

That's why Turman had laughed.

That's why he'd been babbling when the ambulance crew found him.

That's why he was talking about elves and fairies.

Chapter 21

Welcome to Fairy Land

She was dead.

That was the only logical conclusion.

It was either that, or she'd cracked up. That would explain the whirlwind inside a building and the voices in her head.

It might even explain the Doctor.

She'd seen it plenty of times. Colleagues broken by the job. Not by dangers on the street, and there were enough of those, even in Huckensall. No, it was the politics of the station that did people in. The need to get ahead. To get promoted.

Schofield had never minded about all that. She was ambitious, of course she was, but getting her sergeant stripes wasn't the be-all and end-all.

She'd become a copper because she wanted to be like her dad, out in the community, helping people. He hadn't cared about climbing up the ranks either. She wanted to be like him. That's all that mattered.

Well, it was what had mattered before she died.

Because she *was* dead, wasn't she?

She groaned. She'd made the mistake of moving, every bone in her body regretting the decision.

Was that a good sign, or a bad sign?

Pain meant that she was alive, unless the afterlife was one big joke. That wouldn't be fair at all.

She coughed. Another mistake. Her lungs felt like they were full of rusty nails. The cough turned into a choke and the choke turned into near respiratory failure.

She opened her eyes, a simple enough act that turned out to be the biggest mistake of all.

It was like being hit in the face with a baseball bat. A baseball bat made of pure light.

Her eyes burned, like they were roasting in their own sockets. She clawed at them, screaming in agony.

No, she wasn't dead, but she'd definitely lost the plot.

Five minutes ago, she had been on a building site in Huckensall. Yes, it was a building site with its own extreme weather system, but it was largely part of a world she understood.

Now, she was somewhere that made no sense whatsoever.

There was grass beneath her head. The brightest, greenest grass she'd ever seen. She was in a forest, but the kind of forest that couldn't possibly exist outside of a picture book.

The trees were tall, skyscraper tall, stretching up towards a sky that was filled with too many stars. No. That wasn't right. She couldn't see the sky through the thick canopy of leaves.

It was the leaves themselves. They were glittering like stars.

She rolled over onto her back. The bark on the tree trunks was deep dark red. Too deep. Too dark. Each knot in the wood was like a whirlpool, spiralling and yet still at the same time. Fungus crawled all over the trees, literally crawled, moving across the ridiculously red bark like giant ridged caterpillars.

And the flowers. They clustered around the roots of the trees, every colour of the rainbow, and a few she had never seen before. Vivid, stunning colours that made her eyes ache. But that was nothing compared to the smell. She could never understand why people insisted on sniffing flowers. They'd always made her sneeze, full of sweet, saccharine perfume. Here it was worse. It stuck to the back of her throat, thick and cloying. She was going to be sick. She turned over, trying to push herself up on her knees. Her head went into a spin, the sounds of the forest coming from all angles. She could hear everything at once: bugs crawling in the pungent earth beneath her fingers, birds flying through the air, each beat of their wings like thunder, a heart beating like a drum.

No, not one heart. Two. Beating together.

'Here,' said a commanding voice. 'Put these on.'

Something slipped over her eyes. Plastic, cool against her skin. She opened her eyes again, but this time they didn't burn. The sounds of the forest retreated, becoming muted, easier to stand.

'Better?'

Schofield looked up to see the Doctor standing over her, his hand reaching down. She took it, and rose unsteadily to her feet. Her ears popped and she went to pull off the sunglasses he'd slipped onto her nose.

'No, don't take them off,' he said quickly, 'or we'll be treated to more of the retching and the screaming.'

She'd been screaming?

'They're mine, but you can borrow them. You're very lucky. Not everyone gets to wear the sonic sunglasses. They're special, just like me.'

'Special how?'

'They're adjusting your vision,' he told her, 'dimming things down so the world isn't so glary. And while they're at it, they're also projecting a sonic cone around you, filtering out the noise. You can thank me later.'

'Sonic sunglasses,' she repeated, trying to make sense of the words.

'Oh, I love a bit of sonic,' he said, grinning. 'Sonic glasses. Sonic screwdriver.' He patted his pockets, his smile faltering. 'Looks like I'll have to get another one of those. Never mind.' He looked around himself, bending back at the hips to gaze up at the trees. 'Even had sonic lipstick once, although it wasn't really my shade. Gave it to a friend.'

'You have friends?'

He glanced back at her, the grin wider than ever. 'Someone's feeling better.'

'Where are we?'

The Doctor jabbed a finger at her. 'And that's why I like you, PC Schofield. Straight to the point. Just like me.'

He stepped forward, gesticulating as he explained, like a teacher. 'We've jumped a groove. We're in the Invisible.'

'And that is?'

'Fairy land.'

She snorted.

He looked confused. 'Why are you laughing?'

'Because that's impossible.'

'Not impossible, the Invisible. I told you about it, back in Mr Marter's house.'

'I didn't believe you then, and I don't believe you now.'

'Even when you're standing in the middle of it.' He made an expansive gesture with his hands. 'What do you think all this is? Disney World?'

'I don't know. But, fairies? Really? The little people?'

The Doctor gave a disapproving look. 'Don't say that. Really. For both our sakes.'

'Why? What's going to happen?'

'I get it,' he said. 'When you think fairies, you think acorn hats, stardust and little gossamer wings. You can blame the Victorians for all that.'

'What should I think, then?'

'Your worst nightmare, wrapped up in insanity with a bow of utter terror.'

This was stupid. 'I don't believe in fairies.'

He shrugged. 'Doesn't matter, because fairies believe in you, and we're in their back garden now, not the other way around.'

Something flapped overhead, a sudden buzz of wings. Schofield jumped, looking up, but there was nothing there.

The truth of the matter was that she didn't want to

believe what the Doctor was telling her, because that would be one step closer to accepting what had happened to her, that she really had slipped into another world.

'So what about you?' she asked, turning on the Doctor.

'What about me?'

She tapped the glasses. 'How come you don't need these?'

'The forest only affects humans that way.'

'Meaning?'

'I think you know what I mean.'

'You're a troll.'

He looked appalled. 'I'm a Time Lord.'

'And that is?'

'Better than a troll.' He caught himself, looking embarrassed, before backtracking. 'Not better, but different.'

'Definitely different,' she agreed, crouching down to examine a crop of fluorescent mushrooms that had bloomed near her feet.

'Don't touch them,' the Doctor advised.

'I'm not going to. I'm not stup—'

She jumped back up as the cap of each mushroom opened to reveal an eye that peered at her.

'I really don't like it here,' she admitted.

'For good reason,' the Doctor told her, stepping closer and dropping his voice. 'Don't look now, but I think we're being watched.'

'I know,' she said, pointing down at the eyes on stalks.

'Not them,' he hissed, pointing over her shoulder.

She turned, seeing nothing but trees.

'I can't see anything?'

'That'll be the sonic sunglasses. Here, allow me.' He tapped their frame and the world became brighter, not enough to cause her pain, but definitely enough to see the three pairs of eyes that glared balefully from between the tree trunks.

'Still don't believe in fairies?' he asked.

There was a growl, deep and guttural.

She could make out their faces now. Hooked noses, wide mouths, brimming with jagged teeth. Their skin was mottled, the colour of mouldy cheese, their hair hanging in long braids. They were tall, they were rangy, and they looked angry.

'Why don't they attack?' she asked.

'They're working out if they want to play with their food first.'

'That's comforting.'

'Wasn't meant to be. When I say run …'

'I'll be right behind you.'

'One,' the Doctor said, as the first of the creatures took a step forward, its clawed hand resting on the nearest tree trunk.

'Two?' Schofield suggested, as its nostrils flared.

'Three!' the Doctor shouted, as the creatures burst forward, ready to tear them limb from limb.

Chapter 22

Safe Together

Bill glanced at her watch as they traipsed through Boggle Wood. It was half two in the afternoon. The sun wouldn't be going down for another couple of hours, but already the sky was growing dim, thick grey clouds smothering the weak autumn sun.

She didn't know which was worse: exploring a spooky wood in the dead of night, or retracing their steps in this strange half-light. It was eerily quiet. No bird sang in the tall barren trees, no dogs walked their owners along the twisting leaf-covered paths.

Masie stomped ahead, kicking up leaves.

'Not too far, eh?'

The girl didn't stop. She'd been in a grump ever since the Doctor had despatched them on their impromptu nature trail. It was hardly surprising. Her world had been turned upside down; Bill could understand that.

She'd only been a baby when her own mum was taken away from her. She'd never known her, the only memories the ones she'd made up. She hadn't even known what she looked like, not really. There hadn't been any photos, until the Doctor changed all that, heading back into the past, armed with a total disregard for the laws of time and a SLR camera. The box full of photos now sat beside Bill's bed, back in Bristol. Her most precious possession.

She couldn't imagine what it would be like to have your mum with you every day for ten years and *then* have her snatched away. How much that would hurt.

Not only had that happened to Masie, she'd also had to cope with a sudden induction into the Doctor's world, with everything that went with it. The monsters. The terror. The realisation that the universe is bigger than you ever imagined.

All things considered, Masie was doing *brilliantly*. Yes, there was the permanent scowl and the bucketful of snark, but that was just a survival mechanism.

If only Noah could understand. He'd faced his sister's wrath almost as soon as they'd left the Doctor on Bugs Close.

'I thought *you* were supposed to be the expert.'

'Of what?'

'Of leaves and stuff.'

'I never said—'

'You *said* you were top of the class. You *said* you got a sticker from Mr Weenink.'

'I did my best.'

'Shame your best didn't know the difference between an oak and a Rohan tree.'

A rowan,' Bill had corrected, immediately regretting the decision. Yeah, way to go. Like the kid needed to feel any more alienated.

'You thought it was an oak too,' Noah had snapped, not mature enough to let the argument drop. 'You didn't know.'

'I never said I did.'

'Yes you did!'

Masie had huffed. Maybe she knew when she was beaten. Maybe she just didn't want to argue any more. 'Just shut up, Noah,' she growled.

But it had gone too far. Her brother wasn't having that. 'No, *you* shut up. You always think you're right, but you're not.'

Bill had tried to play peacekeeper. 'Hey, hey, hey. There's no need—'

'It's not fair,' Noah continued, shouting over her. 'I'm going to—'

'Do what?' Masie said, whirling around. 'Tell Mum? Good luck with that. She's *gone* and it's your fault.'

The sheer venom in the 10-year-old's voice had stopped both Bill and Noah in their tracks.

'Masie ...' Bill began, but the girl's tirade had only just begun.

'If it wasn't for you and your stupid Shining Man story, she wouldn't have gone out.'

'It wasn't a story!' he bawled back. 'It really happened!'

'Maybe she wasn't taken by a Shining Man at all! Maybe she just wanted to get away from you and your stupid whining!'

'That's enough!' The severity in Bill's voice had surprised even her. *Hark at me, sounding like a grown up. Being around the Doctor must be rubbing off.* Who was she kidding? The

Doctor was the most childish grown-up she'd ever met. Still, it worked. Masie shut up, dropping into a super sulk.

Noah's face had creased up. She'd seen the boy cry plenty of times over the last 24 hours, but this was different. This was sorrow beyond tears. This was heartache.

'Hey,' she'd said, dropping down to pull him into a hug. 'This is no good. Any of it. We need to pull together. We're a team.'

Masie had snorted. 'Is that why the Doctor sent us away?'

'He didn't. He gave us a job.'

'To find a stupid tree. What good will it do, anyway? Why does he always think he knows best?'

'Because he does, most of the time. Anyway, this isn't about him. It's about you; you and your brother. You're both angry and scared, I get that, really I do. But taking it out on each other isn't helping anyone, and it's not going to bring back your mum.'

She'd stopped short of telling Masie to say sorry. That would've been pushing it. Thankfully there was no need. Masie had grunted a half-apology and trudged into the wood.

Noah had sniffed, looking down at the ground.

'You OK?'

'I guess.'

'She's just upset. She didn't mean any of that. Not really.'

Noah hadn't looked convinced as he took Bill's hand and they'd set off after his sister.

Masie still wasn't making it easy. She wouldn't slow down, even after Bill had called out. She kept going off the poor excuse for a path to squeeze between trees or clamber over fallen tree trunks. Bill could have guessed what would happen.

Too far for them to catch her, Masie slipped and let out a squeal. She fell out of sight, and they could hear her rolling away.

'Masie!' Noah shouted, letting go of Bill's hand to rush forwards.

'No, wait!' Bill said, grabbing him before he could drop down the sudden slope that had already claimed his sister.

Masie was lying in a small clearing between the trees, and wasn't moving.

'Are you all right?' Bill said, scrambling down the bank and trying not to go tumbling down the hill like Jack following Jill. The last thing she wanted was a broken crown. Noah, at least, was more sensible, sliding down on his bum with scant regard for his jeans.

'Masie,' Bill said as she reached the bottom.

The girl stirred, moaning. Thank God. She was awake.

'Does anything hurt?'

'No,' Masie whimpered, trying not to cry.

She let Bill help her up, only to have Noah throw his arms around her. She didn't fight the hug, pulling him in close.

'I'm sorry, Masie,' he said. 'I'm sorry I got the leaf wrong.'

'I'm sorry too. But you can't be as good as me.'

'Hey,' he complained, pulling out of the hug, but his sister was smiling, and not unkindly.

The smile fell away when a twig snapped, just beyond the trees.

'What was that?' Masie asked, grabbing her brother's hand and pulling him back towards Bill.

'I don't know,' Bill admitted quietly, putting protective hands on their shoulders.

Down here, the trees were packed closer than ever, the shadows between just that little bit darker. They waited, not daring to move, their hearts thumping in their throats, but all was still. No more movement. No more sounds, except for the gentle sway of the trees, the wood creaking in the wind.

Bill forced herself to relax, giving their shoulders a reassuring squeeze. 'It's fine. There's nothing there.'

'Are you sure?' Noah stammered.

'Yeah,' she told. 'It was just a—'

Leaves crunched into the ground, nearer than before. Louder. There was a grunt, deep and wet, and all three of them scrambled back up the slope, grabbing exposed roots, clumps of weeds, anything to get leverage. Noah was the first to the top, springing up the bank like a mountain goat. Masie was close behind, Bill taking longer, slipping as she reached the path. She pitched forward, grabbing a branch, pulling herself up over the edge.

She looked down, expecting to see a pair of glowing eyes. Instead, a deer stared up at her, dark eyes wide with fear, long legs trembling. It twitched its ears and hopped away, back into the trees.

Bill laughed, relief washing over her. The children joined in, Masie forgetting her mardy pre-teen act and letting Bill pull her in for a hug.

'If you go down to the woods today ...' Bill laughed.

'Be sure of a big surprise,' Noah said, throwing his arms around them both.

'Hey, get off, Peanut,' Masie said.

'Peanut?' Bill asked, looking down at them.

'That's what Mum calls me,' Noah said proudly. 'Her little Peanut.'

'Peanut ...' repeated a voice nearby.

Bill twisted around so fast that she almost tumbled back down the hill. 'Who was that?'

'Mum?' Noah asked. 'Mum, where are you?'

The kids ran forward, Bill following behind. 'Sammy? Are you there? I've got Noah and Masie with me. They want to find you.'

'Masie ...' the voice said. 'Find us.'

'Over here,' Masie said, finding a silver tree. It had grown at an angle; its branches empty save for a few stubborn leaves. The rest were in its shadow.

Noah snatched one up. 'That's a rowan leaf! Bill, it's a rowan!'

Bill skirted around the tree. There was a hole in the earth, like a burrow beneath the roots. 'There's someone down there.'

Masie appeared beside her, nearly falling over in her haste. 'Mum?'

A woman was in the hole, curled up in a ball. Her curly hair was tangled with leaves and bark, her coat and skirt covered with grime.

'Trapped,' she wailed, shaking, not from cold, but fear.

'It's OK,' Bill said. 'We've found you.'

'Found us.'

'Mum,' Noah sobbed.

Bill got down behind the cramped hole, offering the woman her hand. 'I can help you out. We all can.'

The woman grabbed Bill's hand and squeezed tight. Her finger nails were black with dirt.

'That's it,' Bill said, as she guided her out of the burrow.

Masie and Noah stood back, hand in hand, staring at their mum, as if they were afraid of coming near.

'It's fine,' Bill said to them, putting an arm around the woman. She held Bill tight, still trembling. Her eyes were screwed up tight. Why wouldn't she open them?

'Mum?' Masie asked, unsure.

'Look,' Bill said. 'It's your kids. Open your eyes so you can see them. We're going to take you home.'

'Home?' she parroted, her voice croaking.

'Yeah, back to Nan,' said Masie, taking a step closer. 'She's been looking after us.'

'Home,' the woman repeated, stronger this time. Her grip on Bill eased, just a little.

'That's it. Come on, Sammy. Open your eyes and we can get you home.'

'Home,' Sammy wailed, and her eyes opened to blaze like torches. Bright. Glaring. Like the eyes of a Shining Man.

Chapter 23

Chased

Schofield thought she'd been scared before. That time she'd been cornered by a guy twice her size in Wythenshawe. When she'd she realised that her daughter wasn't with her during a shopping trip to the Arndale Centre.

But nothing compared to this, not even the sinking dread of realising that her little girl wasn't holding her hand any more. At least Elsie was safe at home with Martin. At least she wasn't here, being hunted through a forest that broke all the rules.

Hunted by those *things*.

'Boggarts,' the Doctor had called out as they had been chased from the clearing, the creatures on their hills.

'What?'

'That's what they're called. I always think it's better to know what you're being chased by.'

'So you can name it while it eats you?'

'Two thousand years of running and I've not been eaten yet. Happy with that record. Don't expect it to change today.'

'I wish I shared your confidence!'

The Doctor laughed. He actually laughed. She was scared witless and he was leaping over logs and ducking beneath low-reaching branches as if being chased through an alien wood was just another day at the office.

Her legs burned with the exertion, her lungs ready to burst. She wanted to stop, to drop to the floor – to throw up! – but she knew it would be suicide. She could hear them crashing through the trees behind them, murderously close.

She glanced over her shoulder, the sonic sunglasses jogging from her nose. She grabbed them before they could fall. The last thing she needed was to drop out of the Doctor's sonic cone.

'They've gone,' she said, slowing her pace.

'No they haven't,' the Doctor insisted.

'Seriously, they're not there.'

They weren't. The three figures with their long swinging arms and loping gait were nowhere to be seen.

There was a flash of green hide through the trees to the left of them.

'They're playing with us,' the Doctor shouted from where he had sped ahead.

'Cat and mouse,' she agreed.

'Something like that. Although here the mice eat the cats so it might be the other way round.'

'You've been here before then?'

'A long time ago,' he admitted.

'And you got home again?'

'I had a little help.'

'What from?'

Something snarled to the left of her. She turned to see and her toe snagged a root. She tumbled forwards, the sonic sunglasses flying from her face.

The world smothered her, all the light and sound the Doctor's gadget had been keeping at bay rushing in. She was drowning in her senses, her eardrums fit to burst.

Hands gripped her arms. She fought back before realising that the fingers didn't end in claws like steak knives. It was the Doctor, helping her up, shoving something into her hands. The sunglasses.

Fumbling with the arms, she pushed them back on her nose. The glare of the Invisible retreated, but there was no time to sob in relief. The Doctor was pulling her on.

'We need to keep going.'

'Easier said than done,' she wheezed, her legs like jelly.

'This way,' the Doctor said, dragging her down a sudden drop. She slipped, crashing to the bottom, this time clutching onto the sunglasses as if her life depended on it, which it probably did.

Again, the Doctor went to help her up, but this time she batted his hand away. 'I can manage.'

'Are you sure?'

They were standing beside a dazzling stream, the water an ever-changing kaleidoscope of colour. Oranges, greens, blues and purples washed together; a liquid rainbow filled with tiny silver fish that swam against the fierce tide.

'Running water,' the Doctor exclaimed, clapping his hands together. 'Thank you, universe!'

'How's that going to help?'

'The Fae can't cross it,' he said, as if this was something she should know, a fact as obvious as the sun rising in the east, or day following night. 'Fairies, gnomes, Boggarts and elves. It disrupts their psycho-magnetic field. Very nasty.'

'I thought that was vampires?'

'What?'

'The thing about running water. That's vampires, not fairies.'

'Have you ever met a vampire?' he asked.

'I suppose you have?'

'Trust me, this'll work.' He glanced up the incline to the trees. 'It won't take them as long to find us.'

'But how are we supposed to get across?' she asked, looking at the water. 'We can't exactly wade through, not with that current. We'll be swept away.'

'It's not the current you need to worry about,' the Doctor told her.

'Then what is it?'

He nodded towards the water. 'See the fish. Think piranhas, but these ones don't stop when they get to your skeleton.'

'You're making that up.'

'Feel free to test that theory.' He started backing up.

Her mouth dropped open. 'You're not going to jump.'

'It's either that or fly.'

'It must be three metres across!'

'Which is why I'm taking a run-up. Do you always talk this much when you're on the run from a dangerous predator?'

The first of the three Boggarts appeared at the top of

the rise, thick strips of saliva hanging from its jowls as it scrambled down towards them.

'Ladies first,' Schofield said, charging towards the bank and throwing herself into the air. She sailed forwards, arms and legs pin-wheeling, before realising that she wasn't going to make it.

She splashed into the stream, the current immediately taking her legs away from beneath her. She went under, grabbing the side of the bank. Her fingers closed around grass and she pulled herself up, breaking the surface. She gasped for breath, her stomach heaving. The water tasted like honey, thick and sweet.

She tried to haul herself out of the water, but the grass tore away from the earth. The water snatched her away, pain shooting up her legs as dozens of tiny jaws went to work on her calves. Either she was going to drown, or she was going to be eaten alive. One way or another, she was finished.

Chapter 24

Sense of Direction

There was a dull *whumph* near her head, and she glanced up to see the Doctor had made it across the stream without even getting wet. Of course he had. But he also had a long branch in his hand that he thrust into the water.

'Grab it!'

'I'll pull you in.'

'No you won't,' he insisted.

Swimming against the torrent, she got hold of the Doctor's lifeline, grasping it with both hands. The Doctor pulled back, slipped and toppled into the water with a splash.

The branch slipped from her fingers and washed away. The Doctor was floundering in the water ahead of her, all arms and legs. Some rescue attempt.

Something whacked her on the side. It was a large rock, standing firm in the water, the torrent gushing around it.

She grabbed it and held on tight. The Doctor rushed by and she snatched at him, grasping his jacket.

Her fingers slipped on the wet stone, and she thought they would be dragged away again, but her grip held. Spitting water from his mouth, the Doctor took hold of the rock and, ignoring the pain from the fish that were literally making a meal of their extremities, they helped each other out of the water and onto the bank.

The Doctor rolled on his back, gulping for air.

'No time for that,' she gasped, using a tree to clamber to her feet.

'No time to breathe?' the Doctor asked.

'You need to learn to multi-task.'

He pushed himself up, pointing across the fast-running water. The steep bank was empty. 'We're fine. The Boggarts are gone. At least for now.'

'I guess you were right,' she admitted.

He leant on his knees, still fighting to breathe. 'Music to my ears. Although, it won't put them off for long,' he admitted. 'They're tenacious beasties. They'll be finding another way around the stream as we speak.'

'Then what are we waiting for?' she asked, brushing down the sleeves of her fleece. That was weird. They were already dry ... and they were gold!

Her entire uniform; her skirt, vest, fleece and shirt had been dyed a brilliant yellow.

'What the hell?'

The Doctor was appraising his own wardrobe: both his jacket and trousers had a similar gleaming hue. 'Golden thread. John Dee would love that. Instant alchemy.'

She pulled up her sleeve, checking her arms. 'But what will it do to my skin?'

'You probably won't need fake tan for a while.'

'It's not funny,' she told him. 'We've no idea what this place is doing to us, what we're breathing in. You've seen the mushrooms.'

'I told you. I've been here before, and I'm just fine.'

'That's a matter of opinion.'

'Granted, I was in a different body back then.'

'Do you ever make sense?'

'Not if I can help it.' He pulled an old-fashioned fob-watch out of his pocket, and shook it against his ear to check if it was still working.

Schofield was boiling. The water hadn't been cold as she expected, but warm, like a hot bath. She felt like she was burning up and hoped it had nothing to do with her new colour scheme. Peeling off her vest and fleece, she watched the Doctor flip open his watch. It didn't have a clock face, but a digital compass which whirled around like a Russian dancer.

She tied the sleeves of her fleece around her waist like a belt. 'So where are we heading?'

'That's a good question.'

'I know. That's why I asked it. You're the one who's been here before. I'm relying on you.'

He snapped the watch shut. 'Multiple poles. The compass doesn't know whether it's coming or going.'

'But you do?'

He pointed at the rushing stream. 'This world runs differently to yours, but there are a lot of similarities.'

'You could have fooled me.'

'The terrain is largely the same. We're standing in the Invisible's version of Boggle wood.'

'Then why didn't we arrive in the middle of a fairy building site?'

'Because they don't have buildings here, at least not how we understand them. We were in the same spot, but how it looked long before Huckensall village popped up, before humanity started encroaching on ultra-terrestrial territory.' He licked his finger and held it up to the air. 'Luckily I have an unerring sense of direction . . .'

'And an ego to match,' Schofield muttered.

'Oh no, that's far more developed.' He pointed ahead, away from the stream. 'This way.' He started through the trees, taking Schofield by surprise.

'This way, where?' she asked, catching up with him.

He pulled a key on a long chain out of his pocket, and dangled it in front of him as if he was about to hypnotise someone. It was a normal Yale key, the kind Schofield had seen on countless keyrings, with one major exception. This one was glowing. It was only faint, but the metal was pulsing, like a heartbeat.

'What is it?' she said, as he stepped over a fallen branch.

'The key to my TARDIS. She's waiting, back in the Visible. And before you ask, the TARDIS is my ship and really rather clever and would take too long to explain right now.'

'I believe you.'

'If we can reach her location, then perhaps I can persuade the old girl to jump the grooves and pick us up.'

'Sounds like a plan.' Well, actually it sounded like complete nonsense, but it was all she had to work with.

The Doctor smiled at her, displaying what looked suspiciously like genuine warmth. 'I like you, PC Schofield. When you're not about to arrest me.'

'Jane.'

He stopped tramping ahead. 'Sorry?'

'Jane. It's my name.'

The Doctor smiled and held out his hand. 'Good to meet you, Jane.'

'Good to meet you too, John.'

He pulled his hand away. 'John?'

'That's your name, isn't it? John Smith.'

'Ah yes,' he said, continuing to follow his key. 'About that.'

She sighed. 'You're not called John.'

'I had to shut you up somehow.'

'So you *lied*?'

'Not exactly. It's a name I use from time to time.'

'But not actually yours.'

He laughed. 'Not even close,' and then, as if realising that she might find this a tad annoying, added a hurried apology: 'Sorry, Jane.'

She stomped ahead to take the lead. 'You can call me PC Schofield.'

'You don't know where you're going,' he called after her.

'I'm sure you'll *delight* in telling me.'

A howl rang out through the trees; far away, but not far enough. The Boggarts were back.

'Which way?' she asked, their squabble forgotten.

The Doctor pointed straight ahead. 'Run.'

She did, not waiting for him to catch up. The Doctor ran behind, barking directions as they pelted through the forest. Left. Right. Over the log. Mind the branch. Down the slope. Up the rise.

She kept her eyes ahead, knowing that the Doctor kept glancing behind. He'd tell her if he saw the monsters. Probably. She thought she trusted him; *hoped* that she could, even if he wasn't really called John.

What other choice did she have? He was her only way out of here.

'Left at that big tree.'

'They're *all* big.'

'The really big one!'

The Boggarts were closer now. She could hear them crashing through the underground, leathery feet pounding, teeth gnashing together.

She scrambled to the left, following the Doctor's instructions and charging forwards.

'That's it. She's just ahead. Carry on.'

Jane Schofield ran as she had never run before. She had no idea what she was running towards, what this mystical TARDIS actually was, but she couldn't hear the Boggarts any more. Maybe they had lost them. Maybe they could get out of this alive.

She allowed herself to glance back, seeing the Doctor running full pelt, arms and legs not quite working in harmony. But the light from the key was intense now. He smiled at her, and she smiled back.

She never saw the arm reach down to wrap around her waist, never realised the danger she was in, until she was pulled up high into the air.

Chapter 25

Tit for Tat

'I've got one,' screamed a voice. 'Here it is!'

It was a woman's voice, impossibly old and yet implausibly young at the same time; as if a crone and a toddler had spoken in unison.

Jane Schofield was up in the air, long fingers encircling her waist, squeezing just that little too tight. At least, she thought they were fingers, scaly and rough, until she looked down and realised that they were made of wood.

She twisted around in the vice-like grip, looking up at what had snatched her from the ground. It was a tree!

Its arm was a gnarled tangle of wooden limbs wound into a contorted mockery of muscles and sinew, the scales she'd felt on its fingers lumps of coarse bark. It had a face of sorts; a hideous mouth and misshapen eyes formed by slashes across its thick trunk that creaked as it yelled in a sing-song voice: 'Come and get it!'

'Put her down this instant,' the Doctor commanded from below. *Too* far below. Schofield was caught between the urge to break the tree's grasp and the knowledge that she would break *herself* if she fell from this height.

'It's alive,' she yelled down to the Doctor.

'Of course I'm alive,' the tree said. 'What do you expect?'

'Don't worry,' the Doctor called up. 'Its bark will be worse than its bite.'

'Ha ha!' she snapped back, her legs dangling helplessly in her gold-stained trousers. One of her equally gilded shoes had slipped off and was down on the ground. Schofield half-considered getting the Doctor to lob it at the tree, not that it would do much good.

'There's no need for this,' the Doctor continued. Schofield thought at first that he was talking to her, before realising that he was addressing her timbered abductor.

'There's every need,' the tree replied. 'They'll pay me handsomely for this one, and for you too!'

The Doctor stepped back as another gnarled arm swept down to catch him, the leaf-tipped talons raking the front of his shirt.

Schofield wriggled in the giant hand, trying to get to her belt. She still had her baton, she was sure of it. There was also her CS spray, of course, but she didn't know how effective a burst of tear gas would be against something that technically didn't have eyeballs.

'What does a tree want with money, anyway?' she grunted.

'Money? Who mentioned money?' the tree croaked. 'The Boggarts will give me a sun of my own, to warm my branches and no one else's. Then the others will be sorry they ignored me. They'll reach out to me, their leaves hungry, but the nutrients will be mine, all mine.'

Around them, the branches of the surrounding trees rustled, as if the trees of the forest were shaking their trunks in disapproval.

On the ground, the Doctor laughed. As if *anything* about this situation was funny. In the distance, Schofield could hear the baying of the Boggarts. The problem was that the distance suddenly didn't seem so distant after all. Their pursuers were closing in and she had no way of breaking free.

She tried sinking her nails beneath the chunks of bark on its fingers, as if they were scabs ready to be ripped from the fresh skin beneath, but the tree only tightened its hold of her, making it hard to breathe.

Still the Doctor wouldn't give up. 'Can't we come to an arrangement?'

That shut the tree up. It regarded the man in the golden coat with renewed interest, rubbing its gnarly stump of a chin. 'I'm listening ...'

'Excellent. Because that's how things work around here isn't it? Deals? Bargains? I scratch your bough, you scratch mine.'

'You would give me a sun?'

The Doctor started looking through his pockets, as if he expected to find a spare star in his loose change. 'Maybe not, but I could give you something better.'

'What's better than sunlight?' the tree snapped.

The Doctor grinned like the wolf that had got the cream. 'You're interested then?'

'I'm always interested, if the price is right. Tit for tat.'

'I like that,' the Doctor said. 'And you'll like what I have in my pocket. You give me my friend, and I'll give you a companion of your own.'

'Show me.'

'Do we have a deal?'

'Show. Me.'

'You strike a hard bargain. Very well.'

With a flourish, the Doctor produced something from his pocket, holding it up between his thumb and forefinger. Schofield couldn't see what it was. Neither could the tree.

Its hand shot out again, but this time the Doctor didn't even try to evade capture. The idiot let himself be lifted up to look her captor in its distorted eye.

'What is it, then?' the tree asked, peering at the tiny object in the Doctor's hand.

'An acorn?!' Schofield exclaimed. That was it? That was the Doctor's bargaining chip?

'It *is* an acorn,' the Doctor confirmed. 'Plucked from Noah Holland's hair by my own fair hand.'

'What do I want with an acorn?' the tree sneered.

'But this isn't any old acorn,' the Doctor insisted. 'It's from the Visible, the other world. It's unlike any tree in this forest, and it could be yours. You could plant it, nurture it, grow it into a mighty tree, right here, your roots intertwined. Imagine it. Someone to talk to, to watch the birds nesting in your boughs. Not like the other trees, the ones who have ignored you for so long. So, what do you say?'

Schofield hung on to the tree's craggy digits as its cavernous eyes narrowed on the seed. The Boggarts were so close she could almost smell them. This wasn't going to work. She was going to die here, in a world she'd never believed existed, crushed by a lonely tree and all because of the Doctor. She'd never see her husband and daughter again, and it was all his fault.

Without warning, the tree let them go. Schofield dropped with a cry, remembering her training and throwing herself into a roll as she hit the forest floor to stop her ankles from shattering.

The Doctor landed beside her, somehow managing to stay on his feet. Show-off. He held up the acorn like a trophy, the tree grinning from limb to limb as it reached down to tenderly accept the seed with knotty fingers. 'Pleasure doing business with you,' he called up, grabbing Schofield's shoulders as soon as she was back on her feet and steering her away. 'I hope you will be very happy together.'

But the tree wasn't listening. It was already waxing lyrical about its prize, trying to make its neighbours green with envy.

'Can we run yet?' Schofield whispered, recovering her shoe from the ground.

'I thought you'd never ask,' said the Doctor and broke into a sprint. He was patting down his pockets as he ran, becoming increasingly agitated.

'What you looking for this time?' she asked. 'A prize-winning conker?'

'The TARDIS key,' he admitted. 'I must have dropped it back there.'

'Back there?' she spluttered. 'Didn't you realise?'

'I was a tad preoccupied!'

'But the key was telling us which way to go.'

'I know!'

'And it was going to get us home!'

'In theory, yes.'

'What do you mean in theory?'

'It was never a certainty. The TARDIS has a mind of her own.'

Now he told her! 'So, now what are we going to do?' she asked, looking back to see if the Boggarts were still on their trail.

'First we try not to get eaten.'

That sound like a good start. 'And then?'

'One step at a time,' he snapped. 'I'm still trying to work that bit out. But don't worry, I always win.'

Something in his tone didn't exactly inspire confidence. 'Who are you trying to convince?' she asked him. 'Me or you?'

For once, the Doctor didn't have an answer, and that scared her more than any Boggart.

Chapter 26

The First of the Three

The Boggarts tore through the forest, the stink of the woman and the man from beyond hanging thick in the air.

That had been clever, putting the water between them. They thought they had got away, but there was no escape. They would wish they had never stumbled upon the Invisible. They would wish they had stayed at home, with their engines and their machine and their dirty, dirty technology.

Oh, the Boggarts knew about technology. They had glimpsed it through the veil, saw how proud the humans were of their accomplishments, how confident they had become.

And yet they still died. They still wasted away. They were still weak.

That was not all the Boggarts knew. They knew the man did not belong, neither in the Invisible nor the other world. They could smell the wandering on him. He had travelled far, seen much. That would make it all the sweeter, the moment when he realised that his fate was sealed, that he would never run again. The man who followed his dreams, trapped in a nightmare.

How they would make him dance. Until both his feet and his sanity were reduced to bloody stumps. They would feast on his despair, revel in his decay. They would destroy him only when they saw fit, as it had always been.

As it should be.

He would be theirs, to do with as they pleased.

The First of the Three dropped down on all fours to cover more ground. This was a fine hunt. The stuff of songs and sagas.

There were others in the court who had forgotten about songs. They cared only about the Lost, and beat their chest in lamentation. They were full of sorrow and regret, remorse and requiem.

Not the Three. The Lost was of no concern to them. Not when the prey was running. Not when there was sport to be had.

A hand closed around the First, plucking him from the ground.

'Let me go,' he railed as he was lifted high into the air. This could not be. He was the First of the Three. Master of the Hunt. To be ensnared by an Woodling of all the creatures in the Forest? He would have his revenge. He would burn the hateful thing to the ground, rip the heartwood from its trunk with his own hands.

The tree did not tremble at the thought of what the First would do to it; it did not quake. Instead, it sprouted new limbs that swiped at the floor, catching his brothers as easily as wisps were caught in a jar. They clawed at its bark, drawing sap from its limbs, but still it held them tight. It held something else, something small: a seed that was a tiny as it was vast.

'Look at my prize,' the tree crowed. 'It will grow into a fine companion, don't you think? A fine companion indeed.'

Even as the First of the Three tried to splinter the Woodling ancient fingers, he realised that he had lost the scent. Their quarry was gone.

But they would not get far.

No one ever did.

They would kill this stupid tree and resume the hunt.

And then the dance would begin anew.

Chapter 27

Home

Noah was yelling even before they reached the front door. 'Nan? Nan!'

Masie pressed her thumb against the doorbell, keeping it down until the kitchen window blinds moved, Hilary Walsh peering through the slats to see what the commotion was about. She took one look at Sammy hanging from Bill's shoulders and the slats snapped shut. They heard their nan run up the hall, and the door flew open.

Hilary stood on the threshold, momently stunned, not able to process what she was seeing.

'A little help would be good?' Bill prompted. The walk from the woods had been murder. Sammy had been a dead weight in her arms, barely able to put one foot in front of the other. The fact that the woman was babbling nonsense and wouldn't open her eyes again didn't help.

'Something's wrong with her,' Masie told her Nan as Hilary regained her senses and helped guide Sammy into the house. 'Really wrong.'

'Oh my poor darling,' Hilary fussed as they made it into the hall. 'Look at the state of you. Where have you been?'

Sammy stumbled, her foot catching on the step and she tumbled forward.

'Look out,' said Bill, only just stopping Hilary from falling with her.

'Where was she?' Hilary asked, her knees cracking as she knelt next to her daughter.

'In the woods,' Bill said. 'Hiding beneath a tree.'

'Beneath a *what*?'

Masie dodged around her nan, grabbing the phone from where it sat on the bookshelf. 'We need to call an ambulance.'

'Good idea, love,' said Hilary, trying to turn Sammy onto her back. 'Can you do that?'

Masie was already keying in the number. 'Course I can.'

'I'm not sure if they're going to be able to help her,' Bill said, pulling Noah into a hug in a vain attempt to comfort the frightened boy.

'What's that supposed to mean?'

As if to answer her mum, Sammy rolled over and opened her eyes. Hilary screamed in terror as light streamed from Sammy's face, blinding her.

The sound sent Sammy into a frenzy. She clamped her hands tight over her ears and scrambled across the floor, ramming into Masie's legs. The girl yelped, dropping the phone which fell onto her mum's head. Sammy cried out, more in fear than in pain, and scurried into the lounge like a demented spider. She crawled behind a large leather armchair, rolling herself into a ball, her back against the wall. Her head was down against her knees, but this time her eyes were open, blazing like floodlights in the corner of the room.

'Sammy love,' Hilary said, rushing into the room, and going to pull the chair out of the way. 'I'm sorry. I didn't mean to scare you. What's *happened* to you?'

'No, stop,' Bill said, charging after her and putting a restraining hand on the chair. 'That'll just make it worse.'

'I need to get to her.' Hilary's voice was bordering on the hysterical.

'She feels safe back there,' Bill argued.

'She's my daughter!'

'No, I don't think she is, not now. She's more like a frightened animal.'

Bill bent down so Sammy could see her, keeping a little distance so the women didn't feel hemmed in. 'Sammy? Sammy, can you talk to me? We got you home. You're safe.'

'No,' Sammy grunted, keeping her gaze down. 'Not safe. Trapped. Still trapped.'

'You're not. I promise you. We're all here for you.'

'Alone!' Sammy wailed, looking up and blinding Bill with the glare from her eyes. 'Alone for so long.'

Behind them, Noah pleaded with his sister. 'Call the ambulance!'

'I'm trying,' Masie replied, dialling 999. She held the phone up to her ear and then pulled it away to look at the handset's LCD display. 'It's not working!'

'Of course it is,' Hilary snapped, snatching the phone from Masie's hand. The woman listened to the handset and then tried again, three electronic beeps accompanying the sharp jabs of her thumb. The phone went back to her ear, and she frowned. 'Something's wrong with the line.

It's just crackling.' She glanced around the room. 'Where did I put my mobile?'

Here,' said Bill, slipping her own phone out of her pocket. She thumbed in her passcode and passed it to Hilary without getting up. 'Use mine.'

Hilary took it without saying thanks and dialled the number. Again, she was disappointed. 'I can't get a signal.'

Bill scrambled up, taking the mobile back. She looked at the screen. It wasn't the signal. It was the entire phone, the power stuttering on and off.

The lights in the room started flashing too, the television suddenly bursting on, digital static on the screen and white noise blaring from the speakers.

'What's happening?' cried Noah, grabbing his sister who hugged him back.

Bill dropped back down to her knees. 'It's Sammy,' she said, looking at the terrified woman. 'She's doing it.'

The bulb in the light fitting exploded, tiny fragments of glass raining down.

And still Sammy muttered under her breath. 'So alone. Trapped. Trapped beneath. Want to be free. He needs to be free.'

'He?' Hilary asked. 'Who's she talking about?'

'The Shining Man,' Bill realised. 'Noah, it dragged your mum into the ground, right? When you saw them in your bedroom?'

Noah nodded. 'Yeah, into a hole.'

Bill got hold of Sammy's head, so she couldn't pull away. She stared into her luminous eyes, her own eyes watering against the assault of bright light. 'Sammy, is the Shining

Man trapped? Can't he get away?'

'Alone,' Sammy wailed.

'Can you show us?'

'What?' Hilary snapped. 'She's not going anywhere! She's only just come home.'

Sammy lurched to her feet, grabbing Bill's wrist. 'Take you there! Now!'

Chapter 28

An Old Friend

'Please,' Schofield gasped. 'I'm going have to stop. Just for a minute.'

She leant on a tree, snatching her hand away as she felt the bark contract beneath her fingers. 'Sorry,' she whispered, no longer feeling self-conscious about talking to a tree. It was amazing how quickly you adapted to a world where all bets were off.

If only she could get used to the heat. It wasn't like a summer's day at home, or even the dry heat of holidays abroad. She couldn't describe it. The temperature seemed to radiate from the ground itself. She had loosened her collar and rolled up her sleeves, but her blouse was drenched, her mouth so dry that her tongue felt twice its normal size.

Even the Doctor had stopped running, stripping off his coat, which was now hung casually over his shoulder. He still looked like he was on a Sunday stroll, though, his brow annoyingly free of sweat.

'They can't be far behind,' he reminded her as she leant forward, rasping for breath.

'And you still have no idea how we're going to get home?'

'Of course I have,' he said, sounding genuinely aggrieved. 'I'm taking us back to the building site, or at least this realm's corresponding location. If a gateway to the Visible has been opened there once, we might be able to open it again.'

'Might?' she said, looking up at him through strands of wet hair.

'Why are people so down on might?' he retorted. 'Might is good. Might is only one step away from can. Would you rather I gave up?'

'I'd rather you didn't lie to me.'

That stopped him. 'What?'

She stood up, her chest still tight. She jabbed her finger towards a large purple tree, its thick trunk splitting into a fork. 'We passed that half an hour ago. Twice, in fact. You haven't a clue where we're going, because we're going around in circles.'

'No,' he insisted. 'That's impossible.' He turned to view the tree, only able to admit the truth when he wasn't looking in her direction. 'Of course, my unerring sense of direction may have deserted me.'

'No one's blaming you.'

He turned back to her. 'It sounds like you are.'

'Doctor, we were attacked by a tree back there. Who's to say the rest of the forest isn't moving, the paths shifting with every step we take?'

His expression clouded at the thought. 'It's a possibility, I suppose.'

He suddenly looked so unsure of himself. Schofield had the feeling that while the sensation wasn't completely unknown to him, the Doctor still didn't know how to process it. He was obviously a man who was used to winning.

'So,' she said, deciding that allowing him to wallow would more than likely end with them being captured and killed, 'what are we going to do?'

He was about to answer when he stopped, frowning. He turned, looking away from her, and, holding his head back, inhaled noisily.

'What are you doing?'

He sniffed again, looking puzzled. 'Something's not right.'

She put her hands on her hips. 'Just the one thing?'

He faced her, his eyes narrowed 'Can't you smell it?'

'Doctor, I can barely smell anything. The entire place stinks of rotting sugar.'

'This way,' he said, setting off to the left.

He jumped over a small flowered shrub, disturbing the blooms which took to the air as one, scattering like butterflies. Schofield cried out, raising her hand to stop the tiny flapping petals from swarming into her face, but by the time that the strange flock had flown into the sky, the Doctor was long gone.

'Wait,' she cried out, heading in the direction she thought he'd disappeared, although her tired legs meant that she had to squeeze past the now flowerless bush rather than leap it in a single bound. Her trousers snagged on the shrub's thorny branches but she pulled them free, hearing the tell-tale rip of fabric. What was one more tear among friends. Thanks to their new colour scheme, they were hardly regulation anyway.

It didn't take long to catch up with the Doctor, who was still following his nose.

'If this works, we should employ you as a bloodhound,' she muttered, feeling slightly ridiculous for pinning her hopes on one man's olfactory passages.

'Through here,' he said, changing direction without warning and pushing his way through a cluster of tightly packed trees to the right. 'Excuse me, ladies.'

She did the same, grazing her cheek on the bark. Why would trees grow so closely anyway? Perhaps they were huddled together for a gossip, a thought that would have seemed crazy any other day.

Rubbing her sore face, she found the Doctor standing gazing at the very last thing she expected to see.

A camper van was parked in the middle of the clearing, and, if its state was anything to go by, had been for quite some time. The bodywork was badly eaten up by rust, the last vestiges of yellow paint peeling away. Grass grew long around the base, bindweed wrapped around the wheel arches and tarnished bumpers.

And yet the Doctor was approaching the van as if it was an old friend. 'Velma, Velma, Velma,' he said, tutting. 'What has happened to you?'

'You recognise this thing?' Schofield said, peering through windows that were caked in grime.

'She belonged to a friend of mine. Well, an acquaintance really. You met her. Charlotte Sadler, aka Cryptogal-UK.'

'The lass with the phone.'

'The very same,' he said, running his hand along the blemished bodywork.

'And I'm assuming she doesn't work for UNIT, either?'

'Not yet, although they could've done a lot worse. Charlotte was persistent, that's for sure.'

Schofield didn't like the way the Doctor was talking. 'What do you mean, *was*?'

The Doctor disappeared around the back of the van. 'You'd better come and see for yourself.'

He was standing beside the van's door. The paint around the handle wasn't just scratched, it was *gouged*, deep channels cut into the metal itself.

'What do these look like to you?'

The answer was obvious. 'Claw marks. Lots and lots of claw marks. The Boggarts?'

He didn't answer, but instead produced an eyeglass from his pocket, the kind her grandad had used to fix watches. Throwing his jacket on the ground and holding the lens in place with his eye, he bent down to inspect the scratches. 'I thought so.'

'Thought what?'

'The paint around the marks has bubbled, from intense heat. Something got its fingers burnt.'

He tapped a button on the side of the eyeglass. It beeped, and whirred and then sparked furiously. The Doctor stood up sharply, the lens dropping from his face. It landed in the grass next to his feet, and smoked furiously, the smell of burning electrics only just noticeable, almost lost in the sickly reek of the forest.

'Is it supposed to do that?' she asked.

The Doctor blinked to clear his vision, and rubbed his eye. 'I should have thought before activating the spectatropic filter. Technology can be a bit temperamental around here.'

'These work all right,' she said, tapping her sunglasses.

'Dimensional shielding in the hinges,' he explained. 'If that failed, the sonic vibrations would reduce your brains to rice pudding.'

'Now he tells me,' she said, shaking her head.

The Doctor peered over her shoulder into the trees behind her. 'The sonic cone probably means that you can't hear that either, can you?'

'Hear what?' she said, looking behind her, half expecting to see a pack of slavering Boggarts.

'Music.'

The way he was glowering told Schofield that the tune wasn't to his taste.

'Nearby?'

He nodded. 'Not far away.'

He turned back to the van, pulling at the door. It stuck, the sliding mechanism long since rusted solid. He pulled harder, the runners squealing as the door yanked open.

The inside of the van was a wreck. Splintered doors hung from ransacked cupboards, the seats shredded, their padding strewn across a cluttered floor. The Doctor brushed some of the detritus away, revealing muddy footprints beneath.

Schofield felt sick. The prints were far too large to be a human's, and then there were the six toes, each ending in a sharp point. She imagined the Boggarts in there; snarling, biting, dragging the poor girl out of the door. At least there was no blood, not that she could see.

The Doctor stalked away, his face darkening. 'Can you close the door?' he asked, his words tight and controlled.

She tried her best, the mechanism sticking before the lock could click home.

The Doctor stood facing the trees. His eyes had been full of sorrow when he'd seen the inside of the van. Now, they were furious, burning with righteous indignation.

She walked up beside him, not wanting to intrude on his grief. He didn't say anything, but reached over to tap the side of the sunglasses. The soundscape of the forest changed, and she realised she could hear a cascading melody filtering through the trees.

'That doesn't sound too bad,' she commented. 'Quite jaunty.' She was pretty sure she'd never used the word jaunty in her life.

The Doctor went back to retrieve his jacket. He slipped his arms through the golden sleeves, despite the heat. Schofield had the sudden impression of a knight pulling on his armour, preparing for battle.

'You asked what we were going to do, PC Schofield,' he said, straightening his lapels and brushing blades of grass from his sleeves. 'It's time to face the music.'

'And dance?' she offered with a half-smile.

The look he gave her was grave. 'I hope not. For both our sakes.'

Chapter 29

Lady of the Dance

This time they didn't have to walk far. The Doctor led them through the trees, finding a steep bank. It was covered in tall nettles that seemed to sway in time to the music that drifted down from above.

'Don't let them sting you,' the Doctor said, ploughing straight into the nettles to clamber up the incline.

'Why?' she hissed up at him, keeping her voice down. 'What will happen?'

He stopped and looked down. 'At best, it'll hurt.'

'And at worst?'

'You'll turn into them.'

'I'll turn into nettles!'

He continued on his way. 'Stranger things have happened.'

She'd wanted him to tell her he was joking, but had been here long enough by now to know that he wasn't.

Thank heavens she hadn't completely abandoned her fleece. She removed the sleeves from around her waist and slipped it back on, pulling the zip up tight to her neck. Tucking her trouser legs into her socks, she slid her hands into her sleeves and started after the Doctor. The nettles were up to her waist as she climbed, her feet struggling to find firm footing beneath the weeds. She fell forward more than once, throwing up a fleece-covered sleeve to stop herself landing face first in the nettles. The barbed leaves caught on the fibres of her jacket, but she kept going, praying that none of the venomous needles found their way through the many tears her uniform had endured.

She made it to the top of the bank, grabbing a low-hanging branch to pull herself the last metre or so. The Doctor was ahead, hiding behind a bush. Keeping her head down, she ran over, dropping down beside him. The music was louder now and ridiculously compelling. Schofield found herself tapping her hand across her knee in time with the melody. In fact, her entire body was tingling. She felt light-headed, her eyelids drooping as an inane smile spread across her face. She was swaying, laughter bubbling up from deep inside her; a giggle that she tried to control but knew would escape. What was wrong with her? And why did she care? It felt good, whatever it was. She didn't want to fight the laugh, but embrace it. Who cared if it gave away their presence? She wanted to dance. She wanted to dance so badly, even though her legs were cramped and her back ached. Dancing would make it all better. Dancing would make her feel alive.

The giggle slipped past her lips and the world began to spin ...

The Doctor leant across and tapped the sunglasses. It was like being slapped in the face to sober you up. Schofield looked around, disorientated, as if realising where she was for the first time.

'Sorry,' he whispered. 'I needed the glasses to sample a few bars before they could filter out the effects.'

Schofield cocked her head. He was right. She couldn't hear the music at all now, although she could still feel it in her gut, a faint vibration. She thought she should tell the Doctor, but liked the sensation, no matter how scary it had been. 'What did it do to me?'

'Ever heard of mind control?'

'Yes, but it was just music.'

He looked at her askance. 'Just music. Music is primal.' He tapped his chest. 'It gets into a heart, into a soul. Ever seen a film before the score is laid down? The action seems stilted, the emotional resonance not quite there. Add a soundtrack, and you make the audience feel the way you want.'

'But where is it coming from?'

He pointed past the bush, but Schofield couldn't see a thing. A thick mist hung low in front of them, obscuring the field beyond.

'Look harder,' he told her.

'How …?' Even before she finished her question, her vision began to clear. It wasn't that the mist was thinning, somehow she knew it was still there, but the sunglasses were reacting to her thoughts, cutting through the fog.

So that's what X-ray vision felt like.

Shapes were solidifying in the haze. Tall, blocky shadows arranged in a circle. Stones! They were standing stones, each covered in moss that seemed to squirm across the faces of the monoliths.

She could see fires now, braziers mounted on poles, and that wasn't all. There were figures gathered around the stones, dancing and cheering. They swam into focus, and Schofield had to clasp her hand over her mouth to stop herself from crying out.

There were Boggarts, with their rangy limbs and shaggy hair, and giants as tall as a double-decker bus with hairy faces and even hairier hands. Some of the throng were small, barely coming up to the Boggarts' bony knees, with large bulbous heads and stubby limbs. Others were obscenely fat, folds of layered flesh covered in swirling tattoos, ridged tusks curling up from their wide, slobbering months.

Then there were the things that hovered in the air, darting back and forth like wasps ready to attack on a summer day. They bore a resemblance to their Boggart cousins, with the same blotchy skin, and long, clawed fingers. But these had long conical heads cropped with tight crimped hair, and translucent wings that whirred between angular shoulder blades.

'The fair folk,' the Doctor explained quietly.

'They don't look very fair to me.'

'Not in any sense of the word.'

'What are they watching?'

'The Dance,' the Doctor replied, as if those were the most hateful words in the English language.

Schofield could make out a large golden harp, glistening in the torchlight. It was being played by a creature with the body the size of a child and the arms of a daddy-long-legs. Its fingers plucked and strummed the strings, mesmerising even from this distance, until Schofield saw something else in the centre of the stone circle.

Someone was dancing, whirling around and around in time to the music, arms waving, and legs kicking.

She wanted to look closer, and the glasses obliged, zooming in like a camera lens. Were these things telepathic?

She could make out a tattered bomber jacket and frayed jeans. It was a woman, dancing as if no one was watching, lost to the music, her head lolling forward as if it was too heavy for her neck, hair obscured by a black beanie hat.

'That's your friend,' Schofield realised. 'Charlotte.'

'She always wanted the limelight.'

Charlotte turned, facing them as she gyrated in the centre of the ring. Her face was gaunt, the creases deep around her nose and mouth. Her eyes were rolling in sunken sockets, her skin as grey as the lock of hair that tumbled down from beneath her hat

'What happened to her?' Schofield asked, the glasses pulling away for her.

'She's been dancing a long time,' the Doctor replied. 'And will continue to do so until her audience grows weary, or her heart ruptures in her chest …'

Chapter 30

Last of the Three

The First of the Three wanted blood. It wanted to crunch bones. It wanted to make something scream.

They had tried to kill the tree. They'd snapped its boughs and stripped the bark from its limbs. Sap had flowed, and the tree had fought back. The Woodling had smashed the Three into the ground. It had flayed their backs with its branches. Roots had sprung from the ground, wrapping around them like serpents, squeezing tight. The First had heard his brother's neck snap, seen his body go limp as it was dragged into the dirt.

The Three had become Two.

Still the tree did not give up. It raised a gigantic hand and brought it down hard. The scream of the First's remaining brother sent birds flying from the canopy.

When the tree raised its hand, what remained of his brother was still.

The Two had become One.

The First didn't want to die. Roots were creeping up his legs, pulling him down into the earth. He kicked and he pulled and he tore himself free.

And the First had escaped; bloody, bruised and alone. The jeers of the tree still rang in his ears, and the pain of leaving his brothers behind made his heart ache. They would be one with the forest. They would be at peace, but not he. Not until he had his revenge.

The woman and man from the other place. This was their fault. They had done it. They'd given the Woodling its prize, the trophy it had protected come what may. Now they would pay the price.

The First of the Three ran through the forest, slashing at trees, revelling in their innocent howls.

'Where did they go?' he demanded. 'Show me or die.'

And the trees showed him. The stupid, cowardly trees. They pointed and swayed and shook their branches.

And he found them.

The First stopped running, and hid behind a tree, watching his prey.

They were in the clearing where the Dancer's carriage stood, where it had been dragged from the Visible so many seasons ago. The First hated it. The stink of the metal burned his nose, but his anger burned deeper still.

The man who had travelled opened a door at the front of the machine and leant inside. His companion was sitting behind a wheel inside the carriage, following instructions. There was a cough and a growl and the carriage roared, smoke bellowing from its rear. The man slammed the door shut and clambered inside.

Their words were strange, but the First could guess what they meant.

'I'll drive.'

'No, I will.'

'You can get out and walk!'

The carriage spluttered and jolted forwards, weeds tearing from its wheels.

They would not escape again.

He charged from the trees, teeth bared, claws sharp. The man was behind the wheel, his eyes wide as he looked through the cracked window. The carriage veered away, rushing towards the trees, leaving nothing but a cloud of foul-smelling air.

The First leapt, landing on its roof. The metal burned his skin, but he hung on, crawling forward as the carriage bucked and weaved between the trees.

They were heading towards the Circle. Towards the Dance. They would never make it to the stones. He would see to that. He would tear this monstrosity apart to get to them.

A branch struck him in the face, nearly knocking him to the ground. Which one of the trees was that? Had it done it on purpose? It didn't matter.

Still he clung on, even though his blackened skin sizzled and smoked. It hurt so much, the pain stripping away the last of his reason. The First could barely remember why he was here, or what he wanted to kill so badly. But kill he would, whatever happened.

The carriage bucked beneath him, climbing the hill to the Dance. The First tried to hang on, but his fingers slipped, his claws slicing furrows into the accursed metal as he slid back.

He tumbled, the carriage speeding away. He crashed to the ground, rolling through the nettles before coming to rest at the bottom of the slope.

His skin was blistered, and his limbs were heavy. He could barely move as stems sprouted from his arms and legs, tall and slender.

His stems.

Buds burst along their thickening length, flowers blooming to catch the light.

His flowers.

Poison glistened in the tiny needles that bristled beneath the unfurling leaves.

His leaves.

The First of the Three did not think of the hunt.

The First of the Three did not think of his brothers.

The First of the Three did not think at all.

Instead he swayed with the rest of the nettles, moving in time to the music of the Dance.

Chapter 31

Into the Circle

Schofield wondered what the camper van's suspension had been like before it had spent the best part of three decades rusting in a fairy forest.

She was still having trouble with what the Doctor had told her: that a girl she'd seen just yesterday, fresh-faced and young, had somehow been trapped here for years, growing old, when barely any time at all had passed at home. Like Harold Marter, it was unbelievable, and like Harold Marter, Schofield had seen the results with her own eyes.

The van bounced up the nettle-strewn slope, the Doctor revving the engine, yelling at the clapped-out vehicle to keep going. There was something on the roof. They could hear it snarling, scraping and screaming. It had to be a Boggart. She expected a clawed hand to come crashing through the windscreen at any moment, but the scrabbling stopped when the Doctor launched the van over the crest of the hill. There was a strangled cry and the *thump-thump-thump* of a body rolling across the roof and it was gone.

The van landed back on its wheels and plunged into the mist.

'Fog lights,' she barked at him.

'They bulbs have gone!'

He put his foot down and they shot forwards, Schofield anchoring herself against the dashboard and wishing again that her seatbelt was working.

Their arrival hadn't gone unnoticed. The Fae spun around, hissing at the camper van's approach.

The Doctor swerved as one of the fairies swooped towards them, talons outstretched. The creature caught a glancing blow, bouncing off the already cracked windscreen.

The rest of the horde were running at them now, the ground shaking as the giants lumbered forward. A Boggart threw itself at her door, its hand wrapping around the handle, only to howl in agony and let go.

'Every legend has its basis in reality,' the Doctor shouted, slewing Velma to the left. 'The Fae are allergic to iron—'

'Which is found in steel, I get it,' Schofield said, clinging to the handgrip above her head. 'But save the science lecture for another time, and concentrate on driving!'

'Oh, you're no fun!'

He swerved, sending the van into a spin. Velma's backend made contact with a giant's leg. The resulting bellow was deafening, even through the sonic cone, but the Doctor sped on, driving away from the stones.

'Where are you going? She's back that way.'

'You told me to concentrate!'

He yanked the wheel to the left, the van slipping in the mud as it came around in a circle. The Fae scattered out of the way and, for a horrible moment, Schofield thought he was going to slam straight into one of the stones itself.

Instead, he pulled to the right, scraping the side of the van against the monolith.

'Charlotte's not going to like that,' he said.

'I don't think she cares any more.'

The old woman who used to be Charlotte Sadler was whirling like a dervish in the middle of the arena.

The Doctor pulled on the handbrake, sending the van into a sharp spin. The back lurched around, piling into the golden harp. The multi-limbed harpist dived out of the way as the gilded instrument disappeared beneath Velma's wheels, the music lost in a sickening crunch.

Charlotte dropped like a sack of clothes where she danced.

The van veered out of control, the Doctor struggling to prevent it from going into a roll. Schofield closed her eyes, convinced that they were going to run straight over Charlotte's motionless body.

They jolted to a halt.

'Move!' barked the Doctor, trying to shove her out of the way.

'You have a door,' she complained.

'It doesn't work.'

Neither did the passenger door. The lock was stuck fast. Scofield put her foot to it, once … twice … and it sprang open. She scrambled from the seat, the Doctor jumping out after her.

The van hadn't hit Charlotte, but she still wasn't moving. Schofield dropped down beside her, feeling for a pulse. It was there, but weak, which came as no surprise now that Schofield could see her up close. The face beneath the beanie hat was haggard, the skin so thin that it was almost transparent.

Charlotte groaned, her eyes flickering. She began to convulse, going into a seizure. It had to be the heightened colours and sounds of the Invisible. On the way back to the van, the Doctor had explained that the Fae would have used their warped science to keep Charlotte alive while she danced for so many years. Now she was free of the music, she was no longer protected. Her senses were under attack and, in her weakened condition, she was going into shock.

There was only one thing to do. Schofield pulled the sonic sunglasses from her eyes, gasping as she experienced the Invisible without the benefit of their defences.

She pushed the glasses onto Charlotte's face. The effect was instantaneous. Her body stopped shaking, her arms and legs going limp, even as Schofield felt like she was on fire.

'Stop,' she heard a voice shouting nearby. The Doctor. She turned, fighting the urge to throw up, her vision hazy, like looking through a prism.

He was standing between them and the approaching Fae, arms stretched out wide as if he could hold the Boggarts and the fairies and the giants and goodness knew what else back by himself.

'If you touch them,' he yelled, 'you will never get what you want.'

'And what do we want?' asked a voice like nails against a blackboard.

Schofield's heart was racing too fast. Her chest felt like it was caught in a vice, the pressure increasing with each passing second.

'The Lost,' the Doctor continued. 'I know where to find them. At least I think I do. That's who you're looking for, isn't it? That's why you brought Charlotte here, why you brought us.'

'The Lost,' came a cry, dozens of voices at once. 'Where is the Lost?'

'Back in our world, back in the Visible. But I can help you. I can find them, but you must let us go. Send us back, and I will return the Lost, I promise.'

'Why should we trust your word?'

'Because it's all I have left. And it's all that matters. I will trust you, if you trust me.'

'And send you back?'

'Yes.'

'What if we want you to dance for us?'

'Oh, I can dance. I can dance for a long, long time. Longer than Charlotte ever could. Longer than the Constable. But if you make me dance, you'll never see the Lost again. Send me back, and you'll have them here with you, where they belong. Tit for tat.'

'Tit for tat?'

'That's the way things are done around here, isn't it?'

Schofield felt like her brain was trying to crawl out of her skull. She remembered what Marter had said when he had reappeared.

'The colours. The colours.'

How many years had he survived like this, every cell of his body on fire? She wanted to pull the glasses back from Charlotte. She was an old woman now. She'd lived her life, albeit one trapped in a nightmare. Schofield was still young. She had a family, a child. Perhaps, if she took the glasses back, she would survive this. She would see them again.

But she had taken an oath.

I do solemnly and sincerely declare and affirm that I will well and truly serve the Queen in the office of constable …

'What's it to be?' the Doctor asked the assembled throng.

… with fairness, integrity, diligence and impartiality, upholding fundamental human rights …

'Do we have a deal?'

… and according equal respect to all people …

'Why won't you answer?'

… I will, to the best of my power, cause the peace to be kept and preserve and prevent … preserve and prevent …

She couldn't remember any more. The words just wouldn't come. She barely knew her name, or why she was holding a dying woman in her arms. And as for the voice shouting at the monsters … She knew she recognised it, but she didn't know who it was, couldn't make out what it was saying.

'The deal is made,' declared a different voice, a voice that sounded like it shouldn't exist. 'Tit for tat. We will send you back.'

The man's voice laughed, calling back to her. 'Did you hear that, Jane? They're sending us back. You're going home, just like I—'

And then she heard no more.

Chapter 32

SPLINK

'You need to go home!' Bill told Masie and Noah as she helped Hilary carry Sammy towards the end of Bugs Close.

'We *all* need to go home,' Hilary insisted. 'Sammy needs help.'

'Help …' Sammy echoed her mother's words, her arms thrown around both their shoulders. 'Need help. Please help.'

'We're coming with you,' Masie insisted, walking behind, her brother's hand in hers.

Bill could understand it. If her mum came back, she wouldn't let *her* out of her sight either.

'But where are we going?' Hilary asked.

'Trapped,' Sammy wheezed as if that explained everything. 'Show you.'

They reached the end of the street. Night was falling and lights were clicking on in windows, cars sweeping down Brownie Hill.

Bill turned to Sammy. The woman's head was hanging down, her matted hair a curtain in front of her face. Perhaps Hilary was right. Perhaps this was a wild goose chase and Sammy should be back home in bed, or in the back of an ambulance.

All she knew was that the Doctor would keep going.

'Where now, Sammy?' she said. 'Where are you taking us?'

'Trapped.'

'Yeah, you said. But where?'

Sammy's head came up, her eyes snapping open to shine like beacons across the road. 'So alone.'

'Sammy love,' Hilary please. 'Please don't. Someone will see.'

'See where I am ...'

'Yeah, and that you're shining like one of those freaks.'

'Nan!' said Masie.

'Well, she is,' Hilary insisted. 'We don't want her carted off to the funny farm!'

'No, Masie doesn't mean that,' Noah cut in to point over the road. 'Look where Mum's looking!'

Bill followed Sammy's gaze. The lights from her eyes were reflecting on the walls of Harold Marter's house.

'The building site?' Bill asked her. 'Is that where you want us to go?'

'Find me,' Sammy slurred, her head dropping forward again, the lights cutting off.

'Let's go,' said Noah, letting go of his sister's hand and stepping into the road.

'Wait,' yelled Masie, grabbing his shoulder and pulling him back. 'There's a car coming. What's Mum told you about running out?'

They waited patiently as a blue car speed down the Brownie Hill, its headlamps as bright as the light that had streamed from Sammy's eyes. Bill could see that the driver was on his mobile, stupid idiot. If Noah had run out, he would never have stopped in time.

Her theory was put to the test as the driver slammed on his brakes. The car slew to a halt, stopping just before it could plough into the man who had appeared in the middle of the road.

And not just any man.

'Doctor!' Bill shouted out. 'Where did you come from?'

It was a question the startled driver wanted answered too. 'What do you think you're doing?' he yelled, hanging out of his window. 'Jumping in front of a car like that – I could have killed you!'

The Doctor ignored him, whirling around as if looking for something. 'No, no, no, no!' he yelled. 'You were supposed to send us *all* back. All three of us!'

The driver blared his horn. 'Get out of the road, you idiot!'

'You're right,' the Doctor agreed. 'I am an idiot! "Send me back you'll have them." That's what I said. Not send us back, but me. They agreed to the deal I'd set.'

'I'll set you in a minute,' the driver said, opening his door.

The Doctor noticed Sammy for the first time, and stumbled out of the road. 'You found her! Well done!'

Behind him, the driver decided he'd wasted enough time on the Doctor and, slamming his door, raced off.

'How did you do that?' Masie asked as the Doctor joined them on the pavement. 'How did you just appear?'

'Magic,' the Doctor replied turning his attention to Sammy. 'And this must be Sammy.'

'Doctor, I think she's linked to the Shining Man,' Bill explained. 'She's talking for him.' She looked down, noticing the sheen of the Doctor's jacket for the first time. 'What happened to your clothes?'

'Long story,' the Doctor said, crouching down so he could see Sammy face to face. 'So you're speaking for the Shining Man, then? Tell me, what does he have to say?'

She opened her eyes, the Doctor flinching in the sudden glare. 'Help me,' she groaned. 'Trapped.'

'She's got lights in her eyes,' Noah told the Doctor, in case he hadn't noticed.

'Thanks for the tip.' He stood, looking at Bill. 'Where are you taking her?'

Bill nodded in the direction of the new-build. 'She wants to go over there.'

He clapped his hands together. 'I thought as much. Then why are we standing around?' He turned and bounded forward, only to stop dead when a taxi sped past, sounding its horn.

'Doctor,' Noah shouted, grabbing his sleeve. 'Don't just run into the road.'

The Doctor flashed him a grateful smile. 'Quite right, Noah. SPLINK and all that.'

'You what?'

A look of confusion crossed the Doctor's face. 'No. I never understood it either. Bring back the Green Cross Code Man, that's what I say.'

Grabbing Noah's hand, he ran across the road, Bill and the others following. Sammy seemed to be walking better, not dragging her feet as much. Perhaps she thought that the Doctor could help. Bill hoped so too, although there was something she wanted to know.

'What did you mean?' she asked him after they'd all made it safely across.

'Hmmm?'

'About all three being sent back.'

The Doctor looked troubled. 'PC Schofield and Charlotte are still in the Invisible.'

'Still? Is that where you were?'

The Doctor nodded. 'Lovely place, or at least it would be if everything wasn't trying to kill you.' He turned his attention back to Sammy. 'But you want to get back there, don't you? You want to go home.'

'She *was* home,' Hilary snapped, 'until we dragged her out here.' She glared angrily at Bill. 'I should never have listened to you.'

'Not your daughter,' the Doctor told her, not taking his eyes off Sammy. 'But the Shining Man, or as I like to call him, the Lost. That is who's talking to us, isn't it?'

'Home,' Sammy moaned.

The Doctor squeezed her shoulder. 'We'll get you there. I made a deal, and I'm a man of my word, even if it gets me killed from time to time.' He pointed towards the building site. 'Are you back there, in the house?'

'Below,' she said, looking up at the Doctor. This time he didn't blink, but stared straight into the light.

'Show me,' he said, taking Sammy from Bill. He swept her up into his arms, Sammy's hands linking around his neck as she let herself be carried across the walkway into the house.

'Should we be going in here?' Masie asked.

'The place looks deserted,' the Doctor told her. 'And I'm not surprised.'

'Why?' Bill asked as Sammy directed them through to the back garden. 'What happened?'

'A touch of the poltergeists,' he replied, 'or the Boggarts to be more precise.' He nodded towards the outhouse at the bottom of the muddy plot. 'You're in there, aren't you?'

Sammy's eyes were burning brighter than ever, light streaming from her mouth and ears. 'Trapped,' she wailed. 'So alone.'

'And you have been for a long time,' the Doctor said, carrying her through the open door towards the pool.

Sammy looked down into the pit, the light from her eyes picking out a spot on the chipped tiles.

'And the eyes have it,' the Doctor said, indicating for Bill to take Sammy from him. He lowered her down so Bill could support her and then squeezed back out of the outhouse into the garden.

'Doctor?' Bill shouted after him.

'Wait there!' came the response as he made for a pile of tools. He rifled through the workmen's equipment, finding what he was looking for.

Hilary stepped aside, looking more than a little alarmed, when he returned to the swimming pool brandishing a large pickaxe.

'That's it Sammy,' he said, making for the shallow end and skipping down the steps into the empty pool.

'What are you going to do with *that*?' Bill asked.

'Do you like fairy stories?' he said, making for the spots of light on the floor.

'I prefer sci-fi,' Bill admitted.

The Doctor tested the weight of the tool in his hands. 'You would.'

'I like them,' Noah said.

'Then I shall tell you one of my own.'

'Are you sure this is the right time?' Hilary asked.

'Just let him,' Bill said. She'd known the Doctor long enough to know when he was showboating.

'Once upon a time,' he said, lifting the pickaxe high above his head, 'there was a little girl …'

And, with that, the Doctor started to dig.

Chapter 33

A Fairy Story

The pickaxe bit into the tiles with a short, sharp *clang*. The Doctor lifted it back up, continuing with his story.

'The girl had a favourite tree and, whenever she could, she used to scramble up into its branches and hide away from the world.'

Clang. Again, he struck the floor. The tiles cracked.

'What she didn't know was that there was something buried beneath the tree.'

Clang. He was through the tiles now, kicking them out of the way to reveal smooth concrete.

'It was a Boggart who had been caught and trapped hundreds of years before …'

'By the Fairy Finder!' Bill cut in, realising where he was going with this.

The Doctor shot her a look. 'Whose story is this?'

'Sorry.'

'Where was I?'

'The Boggart was trapped,' Masie reminded him.

'Ah yes …'

Clang. Now, the Doctor went to work on the concrete.

'Bound in iron, the Boggart was cast into a deep hole ...'

Clang. Plumes of dust accompanied every strike.

'A tree planted on the spot. As it grew, the roots stretched down into the ground ...'

Clang. Cracks started to appear in the concrete.

'Wrapping themselves around the Boggart, making sure it could never escape. Now, it's hard to kill a member of the Fair Folk ...'

Clang. The concrete around the Doctor's feet now resembled a jigsaw.

'Some would say it's impossible. Instead, the Boggart fell asleep ...'

'Like a hedgehog?' Noah asked.

The Doctor stopped digging and looked at the boy. 'What?'

'Hedgehogs hibernate for winter.'

The Doctor considered this. 'That they do. Good point.' Noah beamed.

'Instead, the Boggart *hibernated* ...'

Clang. The Doctor finished loosening the concrete. He threw the pickaxe aside and started prising great chunks out of the ground. Bill let Hilary take Sammy's weight and rushed down into the pool.

'So what happened to the Boggart?' she asked, dropping to her knees to help.

'It was forgotten,' the Doctor said, lugging lump after lump of concrete out of the hole. 'The tree grew large, and the Boggart slept. But the tree's roots sucked up a little of its magic, keeping the tree alive long past its sell-by date, long enough for the little girl to climb into its branches centuries later. The magic flowed into her. It didn't do her any harm – and thankfully it didn't give her any superpowers. The world's had enough of that kind of thing recently. In time she grew up and had children of her own.' He glanced up at Sammy. 'A daughter called Masie and a son called Noah.'

Masie's eyes went wide. 'The little girl is Mum?'

The Doctor nodded, indicating the hole. 'And the tree used to stand right here.'

The concrete was cleared away now, leaving nothing but compacted earth.

'Noah,' he said, standing up and rubbing his hands down, 'I need a shovel. Can you get one for me? Out where I found the axe?'

The boy hurried out into the growing darkness, returning with a spade that was almost as tall as he was. He passed it down to the Doctor, who returned to the hole and resumed both his excavation and the story.

'A link was established between the Boggart and the girl. She never knew about it, and neither did the Boggart. It was lost in its dreams, until the tree was grubbed up.'

'To build this place,' Bill said, watching him dig.

The Doctor threw a shovelful of dirt over his shoulder. 'The Boggart woke up deep within the ground. All it could hear from above was noise and confusion. It was scared.'

'So scared,' Sammy said, gasping as the Doctor's foot pushed the shovel back into the exposed ground.

A breeze ruffled Bill's hair. The Doctor looked up, alarmed.

'No!' he said firmly, glancing up at Sammy. 'No, tell it we're trying to help.'

Bill staggered. She knew why the Doctor was worried. This was like before, in the TARDIS.

'Just want to be home,' Sammy whimpered as the wind intensified.

'What's happening?' Noah cried, hugging his sister close to him.

Bill was struggling to stand. The wind was blowing them back from the hole.

'It's trying to protect itself,' he shouted above the storm. 'It's scared.'

Masie screamed as lights appeared all around the outhouse. Shining Men stared in through the windows, light streaming from their eyes and mouths.

'I know how it feels,' Bill said.

'I'm trying to get you home,' the Doctor cried out as Bill was blown from her feet to skid across the tiles. The Doctor's shovel clattered to the floor. He had fallen on his back, buffeted by the winds.

Above them, the Shining Men had slipped through the walls of the outbuilding. They didn't walk. They barely moved. They just shifted forward in the blink of an eye.

'I thought the Shining Men were an attack,' the Doctor shouted, crawling back towards the hole. 'Breaking through the veil between the Invisible and the Visible, but I was wrong. They were a cry for help. The Boggart was already here and it was alone.'

'Alone!' Sammy and the Shining Men wailed in unison.

'Even now it can't help it. It has no way to understand what's happening. The Shining Men are manifestations of its fear; its mind splintered over and over again. That's why

242

people feel trapped in their presence, why they feel they can't get away.'

He'd reached the hole in the floor now and was hanging on to the broken concrete.

'When one of its avatars met Sammy, their minds linked, thanks to the special bond they already shared. Meanwhile, across the veil, the Fae heard the cry of their prodigal son. They came looking, but we couldn't understand them. And we were afraid.'

Bill didn't know who he was talking to, her or the Shining Men. He started digging into the dirt with his bare hands. She crawled forward, fighting against the wind, and helped, clawing through the earth.

'It's forgotten what it's like not to be scared. Everything is a potential threat, even the sound of someone trying to dig it out.'

The light from the chorus of eyes shone brighter than ever, reflecting painfully from the swimming pool's white tiles.

Bill looked down, grit and dirt in her eyes. There was something there, in the earth. It glinted in the light.

'Doctor!'

He saw it, shoving his hand deep into the earth.

'That's what fear does,' he shouted, his voice hoarse as he tried to drag what they'd uncovered from the ground. 'It blots everything else out. You can't think straight. Even if someone tells you one thing, you believe the other. Once you give into fear, it consumes you, remaking you in its image.'

Bill plunged her own hand into the ground, her fingers touching something hard and cold. It felt like the links of a chain. She wrapped her fingers around the metal and pulled.

'That's it,' the Doctor yelled. 'Nearly there.'

The wind was so strong now that she thought she was going to be lifted from the floor. She pulled and she pulled, but the thing in the ground wouldn't budge.

'Doctor?'

'Just a little more!'

The light from the Shining Men was intense. She couldn't see anything but the glare, not the Doctor, not her own hand. She couldn't see, she couldn't breathe, and as the wind raged, she couldn't hear.

All she knew was that she was very, very afraid.

Chapter 34

The Final Deal

Bill was thrown back, her hands snatched away from the metal links beneath the ground. She slammed against the tiles, and everything went dark.

She opened her eyes. The wind was gone. The light was gone. Even the Shining Men were gone.

Everything was fuzzy, but the first thing she saw when her focus returned was an arm hanging over the edge of the pool.

'Sammy!' she croaked, forcing herself up. She ran to the shallow end, bounding up the steps. Sammy was lying face down beside the pool. Her children were nearby, wrapped in a protective hug from their grandmother.

Sammy wasn't moving.

Bill turned her over. She looked so pale. Was she even breathing? She put her ear to Sammy's mouth, listening for breath. She wasn't even sure what to do if see couldn't hear anything.

'Mum?'

It was Noah, pulling himself from Hilary's arms. He crawled over to them.

'Mum!'

Bill jolted up as Sammy coughed, a rough, painful hack.

'Sammy love,' Hilary said, appearing by their side, Masie with her.

Sammy's eyes flickered open, but no light streamed out. They were bloodshot and tired, but brilliantly human, even as they narrowed in confusion. 'Mum?'

'Oh love,' Hilary sobbed, pulling her daughter into a bear hug. 'It's you. You've come back to us.'

The children fell into the embrace, three generations clinging to each other and never wanting to let go.

A tear spilled down Bill's cheek as she sat back and let them have their moment.

'Bill.'

The Doctor's voice was soft. He was down in the pool, his discoloured suit covered with dirt. In front of him, curled in a ball, was the Boggart.

Bill ran down to join them. A thick metal chain was wrapped tight around the creature, rusted with age but still as strong as when the Fairy Finder had come to call. The Boggart's skin was scarred whenever it met the iron, the hair of its head full of mud and twigs, as Sammy's had been when they had pulled her from beneath the tree.

And it was crying like a frightened puppy.

'Is it …?'

'It's not dangerous,' the Doctor told her, kneeling forward to examine the creature that flinched even before he came near.

'I was going to say is it hurt?'

'Of course it is,' the Doctor replied. 'Look at it.'

Above them, Noah let out a cry of alarm. Bill realised that the pool wasn't empty any more. It was filled with creatures that crowded around them. Some were Boggarts, all limbs, teeth and hair. Others hovered above the ground on buzzing wings, or hunkered down on the ground, glaring at them with eyes that just didn't make sense.

Bill found it hard to focus on any of them, as if her brain was struggling to believe they were there in the first place.

The Doctor got to his feet to address the visitors.

'I did as you asked.' He looked down at the cowering Boggart. 'I found the Lost. Take him and be gone.'

None of the creatures moved. Instead they held back, their eyes flicking from their bound brother to the Doctor.

The Doctor took a moment and then slapped his forehead in a broad pantomime. 'Of course, silly me. You can't come near, because of the iron. That isn't watered-down rubbish like steel, but atomic number 26, one hundred per cent ferric. I bet it's blocking psychic powers like stone walls block Wi-Fi, not to mention what it'll do to your complexions if you get too close.' He snatched up the pickaxe, holding it with one hand. 'You want me to release him?'

'You promised,' said one of the flying creatures, its voice like dead leaves in the wind.

'No, I'd said I'd return him to you, which I have. That was the deal.'

The Boggart whimpered on the floor.

'Doctor, let it go,' Bill told him. 'Stop being so cruel.'

He ignored her, continuing to stare at the creatures. 'Unless you want to make another bargain.'

'What do you have to offer?' whispered the voice.

'I will undo the chains, if Jane Schofield and Charlotte Sadler are returned to me as they were. It's a simple enough transaction. What do you say?'

'You have our word,' came the reply.

'And that's good enough to me. Of course, this would have been a lot easier if I still had my sonic screwdriver ...'

He raised the axe above his head, and Bill felt her heart jump to her mouth. Surely he wasn't going to –

Clang!

The pickaxe struck the padlock the Doctor had positioned beside his feet. The chains slipped free of the lock, falling from the Boggart.

The creature lifted its head and opened its eyes, which blazed with the fury of the Shining Men. Then it unfurled its limbs like the first snowdrop of spring and rose into the air, long, emancipated arms stretching out after centuries of being constricted. Its lips drew back into a warm, genuine smile that glowed brighter than its eyes, its entire body becoming incandescent.

'Home,' it croaked, hope filling its gruff voice. 'Home at last.'

Bill shielded her eyes as the light flared before fading a second later. The Boggart was gone, as were the rest of the Fair Folk.

Two bodies sprawled where the Boggart had been found. One wore a dilapidated bomber jacket, the other a police uniform, its tattered fabric dyed gold instead of navy blue.

'PC Schofield,' the Doctor exclaimed, dropping onto one knee. 'Charlotte!'

Even in the half-light of the outbuilding, Bill could see that something was wrong. Schofield's hair was brittle and milk-white, while Charlotte's skin was like tissue paper, creased with age.

They were old, like Harold Marter before them. Too old. Their breath wheezed in narrow chests, their limbs so thin and fragile that it looked like a single touch would snap their bones like twigs.

'No!' the Doctor bellowed, jumping to his feet. 'As they were! That was the deal. I took you at your word.'

'And the debt will be paid,' rasped a voice. Bill span around, expecting to see the Boggart behind her. Instead, the voice came from Sammy, her eyes blazing one last time. Her children scuttled back as she rose into the sky, hanging above them like an angel.

'You saved me, Doctor,' the Boggart spoke through her. 'And I will pay what I owe.'

Light streamed from her body, like sunbeams breaking through clouds. Bill jumped back as it washed over the frail bodies in front of them.

'Settlement is made,' the Boggart said, and the light cut off as someone had flicked a switch. Sammy let out a cry, not with the voice of the Boggart, but that of a woman who suddenly finds herself hovering two metres from the ground.

She dropped, Hilary stepping forward to catch her before she fell into the pool.

Charlotte and PC Schofield stirred at Bill's feet. They no longer looked like crones on the cusp of death, but the vibrant, vital women Bill had first met.

The Holland family ran down the slope of the swimming pool and the hugs began again. This time Bill was in the heart of them. Sammy hugged Bill, Bill hugged the kids, Hilary hugged them all. The Doctor leant on the pickaxe and smiled, before a voice from the tiled floor made him laugh out loud.

'Will someone please tell me what the hell is going on?' PC Schofield said, staring up at them all in bewilderment.

Chapter 35

And They Lived ...

'What did you do with the mug?' Hilary Walsh asked the Doctor, who was skulking near the lounge door, looking decidedly uncomfortable.

'The mug?'

'I made you a cup of tea,' she reminded him. 'When you came to look at Noah's room.'

'You left it in Velma,' Bill reminded him.

'Velma?'

'My camper van,' Charlotte said from the leather chair in the corner of the room. 'Guess I'll never see her again.'

'I doubt she'd pass her next MOT,' the Doctor told her.

'That's nothing new,' Charlotte said, still looking shell-shocked.

Sammy knew how she felt. She could remember hardly anything about the last few days, not since she'd run out to confront the Shining Man. There were scraps of memories, but she was pretty sure most of them weren't even hers. All that mattered was that she was home, snuggled on the sofa with her kids.

'Did someone mention tea?' she asked, going to stand up. 'I'll pop the kettle on.'

'No you won't,' her mum told her, springing into action. 'I'll make one for everyone, and then I'm running you a bath, Sammy love.'

Sammy didn't argue.

Her mum bustled from the room, pushing the Doctor out of the way. Sammy still wasn't really sure who he was, other than that he was a friend and Noah *adored* him.

PC Schofield walked in, wearing her peculiarly gold uniform. She handed a mobile phone back to Bill.

'Thanks. A car's on its way. Turman's in hospital.'

The police officer had the same look in her eyes, like she'd just come out of a dream.

'I suppose they'll want to talk to us all,' Sammy said. 'But what are we supposed to say?'

'Beats me,' Charlotte admitted. 'Any advice, Doctor?'

Sammy looked towards the lounge door.

'Doctor?' Noah said, leaning forward on the sofa.

Sammy pushed herself up, walking out to the kitchen. 'Mum, are the Doctor and Bill with you?'

'No, love. They're in the lounge, aren't they?'

Sammy turned to see the front door was ajar.

'They haven't gone?' PC Schofield asked, flinging the door open and looking out on the street. 'How am I supposed to explain all this to the Sarge without them?'

A wave of dizziness washed over Sammy. Her mum was beside her in a flash, helping her back to the sofa.

'Mum?' Masie looked over from where she was passing her mobile phone to that Charlotte girl. 'Are you all right?'

'I'm fine,' Sammy insisted. 'I promise.'

Of course she was. She was home.

'I could have done with a cup of tea,' Bill complained as they trudged through the wood.

'We have tea,' the Doctor told her. 'A whole room of tea. Straight on past the boot cupboard and second door to the right.' He paused. 'Or is that the observatory? Anyway, it's all in there. Earl Grey. Darjeeling. PG Tips …'

He held a branch aside so that she could continue along the path, apologising to the tree as he let it swing back.

'Or you could wait until we get back to Bristol. You know how Nardole likes to fuss around you. I bet he can even find some Battenberg.'

She pulled a face. 'Ugh! Can't stand the stuff.'

'There's no accounting for taste.'

'What about this place?' Bill asked as they found the TARDIS exactly where they left it.

He paused by the door. 'What about it?'

'Are they gone now? The Fae?'

He looked around at the trees, sniffing the air. 'The veil has been secured again. The barrier only lowered thanks to all the fear generated by the Shining Men craze. That's how the ultra-terrestrials could slip back and forth. I doubt they'd want to come back for a while.'

'And the Shining Men? The fake ones, I mean.'

'Oh, they'll be forgotten soon enough. Some other nonsense will replace them online.' He patted down his pockets, looking for the key. Then he stopped and sighed.

'What's wrong?'

'The key's still in the Invisible,' he told her mournfully.

Bill couldn't believe what she was hearing. 'Then how are we supposed to get back into the TARDIS?'

He smiled and clicked his fingers, the TARDIS door snapping open behind him. 'Magic?'

She smiled, shoving him into the control room. 'Show off.'

Boggle Wood reverberated to the unearthly sound of the TARDIS engines. The noise faded away and with it the police box.

'Gotcha!' said Charlotte from behind a tree. She pressed the red button on Masie's camera app and checked the footage. On screen, the Doctor and Bill got into the TARDIS and the blue box disappeared.

She paused the video and smiled.

This was going to go viral …

Acknowledgements

My thanks go to Justin Richards, Charlotte Macdonald and Albert DePetrillo for making my childhood dream of writing a Doctor Who novel a reality.

Thanks also to Edward Russell for giving me a sneak peek of Bill on screen, George Mann and Mark Wright for keeping me sane during writing, my agent Jane for keeping everything ticking along, my fellow authors Mike and Jonathan for our mutual support group and Andrew James for giving me a little time off from the Ninth Doctor to concentrate on the Twelfth.

And also, thank you to my wonderful family, to Clare, Chloe and Connie, for supporting me as I hammered away at the keyboard and babbled on about fairies and boggarts. Love you.

Ⓒ 4/8/19